Why is Kristyn A. Kutter?

Normandy D. Piccolo

NBI

Normandy's Bright Ideas
Florida

Why is Kristyn A. Kutter?
Printed in the United States of America
Copyright ©2019, 2023 by Normandy's Bright Ideas
ISBN: 978-0-9979349-5-3

Pixabay.com Photos Credits:
Alexandr Ivanov
Gerd Altmann
Alexas Fotos

www.normandydpiccolo.com

Why is Kristyn A. Kutter? won two awards and was placed in the TOP 10 List for Fiction/Non-Fiction and the Fiction Recommendation List.

2021 In the Margins Book Award/ School Library Journal

TRIGGER WARNING

Why is Kristyn A. Kutter? discusses serious and difficult issues regarding self-harm, depression, and suicide. If you or anyone you know are struggling with any of those issues, please seek help at a support or crisis center in your area or online through local and national organizations.

National Alliance on Mental Illness (NAMI)
800-950-6264(NAMI)
info@nami.org
Text "NAMI" to 741741

Suicide Prevention Lifeline
800-273-8255

Includes strong language, non-graphic depictions of self-harm, drug and alcohol usage and sexual situations. Recommended for ages 16+*.

SELF-HARM IS NEVER THE ANSWER.
SUICIDE IS NEVER THE ANSWER.

"This cut is for..."

Kristyn Amelia Kutter

Location, New York City.
Born of British American parents.

Beautiful, but awkward.
Fragile, yet able.
Lost, but still somehow existing.
Happiness - a long-forgotten sentiment.

Headstrong, yet submissive.
Crass, but delicate.
Consumed with vulnerability.
Persistently fearing emotional intimacy.

A peppered British and North American accented voice.
A wicked flirtatious laugh.
A smirk *always* displayed upon the face.
A daredevil who will try anything, except *Fugu*.

Secretive, yet sometimes forthright.
A truth seeker, but a liar, too.
Honest feelings often hidden behind sarcastic remarks.
Pain masked using drink, drugs and self-harm.

A master of illusion.
But, also a failure at acknowledging her own delusions.
Believing herself to be clever and in control.
Allowing one to see only what she is willing to reveal.
Nothing more.

Petite.
But, not too short.
Slender.
But, not overly thin.

She has porcelain skin, dark hair and smells of coconut.
Light pink lip gloss hides her naturally plump, pursed lips.
Both sapphire blue eyes coated with smudged black eyeliner.
Hints of light peach blush coat her strong cheek bones.

She always wears frayed hem, bootcut, ripped jeans.
A black long-sleeved burnout T-shirt with the collar cut off,
loosely hangs off her boney right shoulder.
Burnout fabric means to her, *'I exist, but not really'*.

Graffitied red sneakers hide her size 6 feet.
They're littered with vile words and band names in black ink.
She removes the right sneaker.
It drops to the floor.

The word *slag* scribbled on the left shoe catches her eye.
She angrily throws the sneaker across the room.
Her bare feet and painted dark blue toenails are now exposed.
The only hidden part of herself she is willing to reveal, so far.

Most think they know her.
They do not.
She does not even know herself.
"Want to know me? Fuck off!"

A faded-red antique wing armchair cradles her tiny frame.
She glances down at her cellphone and scowls.
Another rumor about her has landed on social media.
She mutters, *"Wankers!"* and slams the phone down.

She pulls both knees in towards her chest and hugs herself.
Vibes of nervousness begin to encroach.
The room feels cold, lifeless – a kismet vibe to her soul.
She shudders and lights a cigarette.

Her eyes scan the room.
Boring furniture and four drab painted walls.
There is a lone spider plant in need of watering.
A cricket trapped inside a floor vent can be heard chirping.

A digital audio voice recorder rests on a table before her.
A hand reaches forward and pushes the *record* button.

chapter one

A feminine, soft-spoken American accented voice begins speaking.

Q.   "Testing. Testing."

Kristyn inhales a drag off her cigarette and replies in her mixed accent.

A.   "'S working."

Q.   "How do you know?"

With cigarette in hand, Kristyn points at the device.

A.   "The red button 's lit."

The playback button is pushed, and the recorded 'testing' is heard.

Q.   "*Ah*, so, it is. Still getting used to this thing."

The record button is pushed again.

Q.   "Let's begin, shall we?"

Kristyn inhales a deep breath then, slowly exhales. She senses her sarcastic defense mechanism already kicking in before the first question is even asked.

She takes one more drag off her barely smoked cigarette before dropping it into a soda can.

Q. "Who are you?"

Kristyn shrugs her shoulders.

Q. "Is there something about yourself you wish to share?"

Kristyn scoffs. She decides to test the boundaries and see what she can and cannot get away with.

'Let's see how you react to this one.'

A. "Here's a clue 'bout me."

Q. "Okay."

A. "I'm Miss Scarlett, chattin' up Colonel Mustard in the Conservatory, while smoking some spliff."

She then smirks.

A. "Satisfied?"

Q. "Interesting."

A. "Which part?"

Q. "I thought you were Kristyn sitting in a chair deliberately avoiding giving my question a serious answer."

Kristyn arch's her eyebrows.

'*Ah, a challenge. I think I might just fancy these sessions.*'

A.   "What if I am?"

Q.   "We have a lot to cover. The sooner you answer my question…"

A.   "The sooner I can get the hell out of here?"

Q.   "Not exactly."

Kristyn glances around the room before returning her gaze forward.

A.   "What do you want to know 'bout me?"

She leans forward and lowers her voice.

A.   "*If I'm super wicked? A mega bitch? Prude with the girls?*"

She then wiggles her bare shoulder in a teasing manner.

A.   "*Loose with the boys? What?*"

Q.   "How about starting with your name and go from there."

Kristyn sighs.

'*Well, this just went from challenging to boring. Fine. We'll do it your way, or I might never get to leave.*'

A.   "I'm Kristyn Amelia Kutter. Age seventeen and three-quarters. I drive a 1975 mauve VW Beatle. I make stupid decisions. But I am smart enough to be taking college courses while still in high school. I hate brussels sprouts. Oh, and I can't stand talking 'bout myself. Ever."

She smirks.

A. "Are we sorted?"

Q. "No."

A. "Too bad. I'm leaving."

Kristyn reaches for her brown fringe cross body purse and gets up from the chair.

Q. "Sit. Back. Down. Please."

Kristyn hesitates. She wants to run away from the room, but even more from herself. Only she cannot seem to force her feet to take a step towards the door. So, she grudgingly plops back down into the chair.

A. "This is shit."

She then slams her purse hard onto the table.

Q. "I detect insolence in your voice."

A. "*Um*, because there is."

Q. "Are you not ready to do this?"

Kristyn looks at the door. She imagines herself leaping out of the chair and running away, leaving her purse, her shoes, her phone — everything behind.

'Oh, how I want to bail. Badly. But I can't. I mean, I can, but I can't. Grr. Why are issues so damn annoying? Or maybe it's just me. Maybe I'm the annoying one.'

A.   "Let's get on with it."

Her eyes lock on the door again.

Q.   "Do you have somewhere else to be?"

A.   "Not really."

Q.   "Then why are you in such a rush to leave?"

A.   "Because any place else is better than being here."

Q.   "Why?"

A.   "Just 's."

Q.   "No one is making you stay."

'Bollocks. You are. Okay. Okay. Maybe I am, too There. I owned it. Satisfied?'

Kristyn turns her gaze from the door to the window. She watches the wind playfully tease dangling leaves on a tree.

Q.   "These sessions are to help you deal with your issues, Kristyn."

She mutters.

A.   "Brilliant."

Q.   "If you choose to be difficult about things, you are not only
      wasting my time, but yours, too."

*'My entire life is a waste of time. So, fucking off more time in sessions doesn't
really matter, right?'*

Her blue sapphire eyes fixate back on the door, again.

Q.   "Why do you avoid talking about yourself?"

Kristyn shrugs her shoulders.

A.   "No point, really."

Q.   "The truth, please."

'It's one version.'

A.   "Fine. I don't like talking 'bout myself. I told you already.
      Apparently, you don't listen very well, do you?"

Q.   "Why do you not like talking about yourself?"

A.   "*Umm*…I'm not a narcissist."

Q.   "Talking about yourself, especially when getting help, does
      not make you a narcissist."

A.   "I disagree."

Q.   "Do you want to know what I think?"

*'Not really. But I have a feeling you're going to tell me anyway despite
my protesting.'*

A. "What?"

Q. "I do not believe…"

She rolls her eyes.

'Here we go.'

Q. "I do not believe concerns about narcissism or a dislike of talking about yourself are the reasons why you work at dodging the topic of 'you'."

Kristyn crosses her arms and scowls.

A. "Are you calling me a liar?"

Q. "More like an avoider."

'I'm currently trying my best to avoid answering your annoying, meaningless questions. It's not working.'

Despite being annoyed, an ounce of her becomes a little curious.

A. "What am I avoiding? I mean, according to you because personally, I don't give a shit."

She then spitefully adds.

A. "For the record."

Q. "I believe you are avoiding self-discovery."

She cranes her neck back and scoffs.

A.   "Self-discovery?"

She snickers.

A.   "That's your amazing answer?"

She is now angry at herself for being curious enough to ask.

'You should have kept your mouth shut. Idiot.'

Q.   "I think you are afraid to discover who Kristyn Amelia Kutter truly is. Could I be right?"

Kristyn shrugs her shoulders.

A.   "I don't know. And, I don't care to know, either."

'You do know, and you do care. Stop lying.'

Q.   "I think you care, or you wouldn't be here."

Kristyn bites down hard on her bottom lip. She winces from the pain at first, before a rush of calm washes over her.

Typical self-harming behavior: to seek physical pain to get immediate relief from emotional distress.

A.   "It doesn't matter who I am in this gutted existence you call life."

'Psst. I already know who I am. A loser. If you were smart, you would have figured it out already and saved us both a lot of time.'

Q.   "Why do you think you do not matter?"

A. "What makes me *not* think it? Can we talk 'bout something else? This whole *'getting to know Kristyn'* chat is getting tiresome."

Kristyn runs her hand through her hair.

Q. "It is important for you to know who you are to heal."

'Request denied. Why am I not surprised?'

A. "Why does it matter who I am? I don't care who you are."

Q. "Because you matter."

A. "Yeah, until this session ends. Then, I'll be a file 13."

Kristyn points her index finger straight ahead.

A. "You know it."

She then points back at herself.

A. "I know it."

Q. "Is that how you see yourself? A file 13?"

A. "Pretty much. Rubbish. Garbage and the like."

Q. "Why do you think you feel this way about yourself?"

Kristyn shrugs her shoulders.

A. "I don't know."

Q.   "Stop saying *'I don't know'*. Be honest. You do know."

A.   "You want me to be honest?"

Q.   "It would help."

'Just remember. You asked. I tried to spare you the agony of hearing my pathetic life's story.'

A.   "*They* think I'm shit. I happen to agree."

Kristyn then scrunches up her face like she bit into a lemon.

'Happy now?'

Q.   "Who are *they?*"

Kristyn begins picking at her fingernails.

A.   "Everyone."

Q.   "Everyone?"

A.   "Yeah. *Everyone.* What part of *everyone* don't you understand?"

'And here I am thinking I'm an idiot. Nice to know in some way I'm not alone.'

Q.   "Can you be more specific?"

Kristyn releases a sigh laced with annoyance while continuing to pick at her fingernails.

A. "Kids at school. Family. Strangers. You know, *everyone*."

Q. "I am confused."

She stops picking at her fingernails and looks up, perplexed.

A. "Seriously?"

Q. "Yes."

A. "Maybe I should be asking the questions then and not you."

Q. "Sorry?"

An alert sounds off on Kristyn's cell phone. The hangnail she had been working on is shoved to the side, as she mutters under her breath, while typing at the same time.

A. *"How in the fuck would you and your wee willy know anything at all 'bout my shagging skills? Little liar!"*

Q. "Please put your phone away."

She adds repeated exclamation points after 'Little Liar!!!!!!!!!!' before slamming the phone down.

A. "Sorted."

Q. "You seem upset by whatever you just read on your phone."

A. "Like I said. *Everyone* thinks I'm shit."

Q. "Not everyone is bad, Kristyn."

She launches into a rant.

A. *"They* are. *They're* soulless. *They* won't leave me alone. It's like *they* want me six feet under getting ravished by worms until there is nothing left but bones sucked dry of marrow. Then, *they* want to torture my bones until each one is reduced to powder, and it still won't be good enough."

Q. "Someone's negative opinion of you is just that. Their opinion. It does not mean it is true."

She rolls her eyes in disbelief.

A. "Why? Because 'Psych-101 for Dummies' said so?"

Q. "Is there anyone in your life who you feel does not view you as …."

A. "Shit?"

Kristyn pulls both legs in and gives herself a hug. She whispers a quiet reply.

A. *"Not anymore."*

chapter two

Q. "What about letting someone in?"

Kristyn shudders at the thought.

A. "No way."

Q. "But you have let people in before, right?"

When most people reflect on past relationships, they see a Norman Rockwell painting. Not me. My encounters tend to favor the brush strokes of Salvador Dali – mostly distorted and very confusing.'

She sneers.

A. "We all make mistakes."

Q. "Are you afraid to let someone in now?"

'Every time I let someone in, I get headfucked. It's just not worth it.'

Q. "Does getting close to someone scare you?"

A. "N-no."
She crosses her arms tightly.

'LIE.'

Q. "Your protective body language tells me people have caused you great pain."

What does your Magic 8 Ball say? I'm guessing, 'Signs point to, yes'.'

She quickly snaps back.

A. "Life has caused me pain."

Q. "We all experience pain in life."

A. "Doesn't make it right, especially when it's done on purpose."

Q. "The mistrust you feel towards others will not disappear until you are willing to trust someone again."

'Perhaps when hell freezes over then I'll give trust some consideration.'

Q. "Will you think about what I said?"

She becomes agitated.

A. "I just want to be left alone. Fuck's sake!"

Q. "Have you ever tried setting boundaries to protect yourself from getting hurt?"

She half-laughs.
A. "Should I draw a chalk line that no one dare try and cross like back in Primary School?"

Q. "You have a metaphoric chalk line drawn already."

A. "Is that so?"

Q. "But I do not believe it to be an actual boundary."

A. "What is it then?"

Q. "A wall."

A. "A wall?"

Q. "I think you try and keep people away because you have a fear of getting hurt again."

A. *"Bugger."*

Q. "Boundaries are not a dreadful thing, Kristyn."

'Easy for you to say because you're not standing in my shoes.'

Q. "Boundaries let people know what you will and will not tolerate."

A. "How do I set a boundary for life then? Can you answer me that? Because I can't stand anything 'bout it anymore."

Dear Life,
You suck! I quit!

Piss off!

chapter three

Kristyn's cell phone beeps and a vinegary expression appears on her face.

'Oh, we're quite the crafty rhymer, aren't we?'

The posting: Kristyn Kutter is a SLUT-DUR!

She rereads the nasty comment in silence.

'So, not only am I slut. But a dumb one, too. Nice.'

A.   *"Ugh!* It never stops."

Q.   "What never stops?"

She remains fixated on her phone.

A.   "Rumors."

'I need to put this dozy cow in her place. Come on, Kristyn. Pull your head out of your bum and think, girl. Think!'

No smart retort comes to mind.

'Maybe she's right. Maybe you are a dumb slut.'

Q.   "Who is treating you …"

She cuts in.

A. "I'm 'bout to find out."

Kristyn soon learns who is hiding behind the unoriginal screenname, FearlessQueenofMean.

A. "That *bitch* doesn't even go to my school."

'I really want to curl up in a ball right now and cry. I'm so bloody tired of fighting. But I can't quit. I just can't. Not, yet anyway.'

Q. "Have you tried blocking people who troll you online?"

Her attention remains on her phone.

A. "Useless."

Q. "Why is it useless?"

A. "*They* just come back 'round with a new fake account."

Q. "Do you enjoy the negative attention you get on social media?"

She looks up.

A. "What? No!"

Q. "Does it make you feel included since you feel ignored by your peers?"

She looks up again with a stunned expression upon her face.

A. "No!"

Q. "Why are you not pickier about who you allow onto your social media pages?"

A. "If I get a friend request from someone, it's hard to reject it."

Q. "Why is it hard for you to refuse a friend request, especially from someone you either do not know or suspect is a troll?"

A. "Because the number of followers on your page matters. It's like a popularity thing. You wouldn't understand."

She resumes looking at her phone.

Q. "So, for you it is about quantity not quality."

She replies without looking up.

A. "*Everyone* else, too."

Q. "Why do you think you have difficulty setting boundaries to keep people from mistreating you?"

'You don't understand. It's hard to crave acceptance and get none. You have no choice but to convince yourself you prefer being alone to keep the pain away. But it's a lie. Nobody likes to be alone — not all the time, anyway. Anyone who says otherwise is full of shit.'

A. "Maybe I'm just stupid."

Q. "You are not stupid, Kristyn."

'Lie.'

A. "People *love* to spread crap 'bout me, true or not."

Q. "Why do you suppose that is?"

Kristyn holds up her cell phone.

A. "I guess the bigger the jerk you are, the more popularity you gain. It's really fucked up, right?"

Q. "Have you considered deleting your social media accounts to avoid being trolled?"

'No. Apparently I'm a masochist.'

A. "I have to be in the know, even if I'm getting socially slammed by *everyone*."

Q. "Does being trolled online make you feel included?"

She scoffs.

A. "I told you already. I prefer being alone."

'You are so full of it, Kristyn. You do not prefer being alone — especially since 'he whose name you cannot utter without losing your shit in tears and gorging down a dozen donuts' left. Hence the now endless parade of nameless, faceless blokes in and out of your bed, as you attempt to use your fanny to try and detract from the pain inside your broken heart.'

Q. "Do you really believe that?"

She does not answer.

Q. "Kristyn?"

A. "What?"

Q. "You did not answer my question."

She plays coy.

A. "What was your question, again?"

Q. "Do you like being alone?"

Kristyn deliberately ignores the question, again. She picks her phone up and finally replies to FearlessQueenofMean's cruel posting.

'STFU!!!!!!!'

She releases a sigh of displeasure, before setting the phone back down.

'Total vanilla response. I suck.'

Kristyn crosses her right leg over her left and begins moving her right foot in small, counterclockwise circles. Tension is beginning to grow.

A. "You know, my Grandpa told me when a baby chick 's born with a spot on its head, the other chicks attack it because it's different. All it takes 's one bird to start pecking at it, and then the rest join in not knowing why they are attacking it, too."

Q. "Do you see yourself as a spotted baby bird?"

She nods her head once.

Q. "Are you basing this opinion of yourself on what others think of you? Or is this how you feel about yourself without any outside influence?"

That's like saying Potato vs Poe-ta-toe. Or Tomato vs. Toe-ma-toe.
It's the same damn thing. Just depends on how you look at it.'

A. "I don't know. Maybe both."

Q. "Why do you choose to believe the hateful things spoken about you, especially if you know they are not true?"

Her phone alerts. A quick look and she sees FearlessQueenofMean fired back a response to her reply.

Q. "Please put your phone away."

She reluctantly complies.

Q. "Back to my question."

She mutters like a pissed off brat.

A. *"Of course."*

Q. "Why do you choose to believe the hateful things spoken about you, especially if you know they are not true?"
A. "I just do."

Q. "I think you can give a better answer than that."

Nothing I say is going to be a good enough answer for you is it?'

She tries again, anyway.

A.   "I'm a failure at everything I try and do in life."

She then flashes a smile devoid of humor.

A.   "Good enough answer for you?"

Q.   "This is not a test."

'Maybe not, but you're making me testy.'

A.   "If you say so."

Q.   "Why do you see yourself as a failure?"

'How do I not see myself as a failure, I think, is the better question. I mean, don't you listen? Don't feel bad if you don't. Nobody else listens to me either.'

A.   "I just don't fit in."

'I don't care to, either.'

Another lie she tells herself to help lessen the sting of social rejection.

A.   "*The Posh Miss Perfects'* can piss off far as I'm concerned!"

'Always with their noses in the air, constantly posting duck lip — boob flaunting photos on social media. Total stuck-up wannabe models.'

Q.   "Are the *'The Posh Miss Perfects'* a band at your school?"

Kristyn laughs.

'Hardly!'

A.   "Only if a nail file constitutes as a musical instrument."

Q.   "I see."

A.   "*They're* a popular clique of girls who go to my school. Perfect hair. Perfect teeth. Perfect clothes. Perfect boyfriends. Perfect family. Perfect friends. Perfect life."

She ends with a snide remark.

A.   "Perfect *twats*."

Q.   "Those girls you believe to be perfect are probably going through a lot of the same issues you are."

Kristyn rolls her eyes.

'Just stop right there.'

Q.   "No one is perfect, Kristyn."

A.   "*They* think *they* are. I think perhaps *they're* right."

'Wow! Maybe the hatred for myself is something The Posh Miss Perfects and I have in common. I wonder if they would invite me to sit with them at their reserved cafeteria table. I could wow them with my vast knowledge of acetone vs non-acetone nail polish remover.'

She replays the thought.

'Okay, Kristyn. I think you've sniffed too much nail polish remover if you think that is ever going to happen. Why would you want it to happen? Are you that desperate for friendship, you'd be willing to suck up to the Posh Miss Perfects?'

She ponders.

'No way! It's better if I keep to myself. Besides, I think I may have screwed around with a few of their boyfriends out of spite. Shhh!'

Q. "The way you think appears to be a bit skewed, Kristyn."

She bows up in the chair like an angry cat whose fur got rubbed backwards.

A. "So now I'm not allowed to have an opinion?"

Q. "Of course, you can have an opinion."

A. "But you just said it was messed up."

Q. "I said your *thinking* was skewed."

A. "What does that mean?"

Q. "Mislead."

A. "Huh?"

'Congratulations, Kristyn! You're now a dumb slut who avoids and is mislead. Three out of three. Cheers!'

Q. "I would like for you to consider changing how you see things."

A. "I see things how they are."

Q. "Why not try and see things in a more positive light verses a negative one, *hmm*?"

A. "You want me to think like *everyone* else. 'S that what you're saying?"

Q "I want you to be yourself, but with eyes of positivity."

A. "If I do that, then I won't be myself."

Q. "Does change frighten you?"

'Hell, YES it does!'

A. "No."

And the lies just keep coming.

Q. "It is never too late to change."

A. "But what if it is?"

chapter four

Kristyn plops down in the chair. She is feeling completely withdrawn.

Q.   "What do you want to talk about today?"

She lights up a cigarette, takes a deep drag and exhales.

A.   "Nothing."

She puts her earbuds in and pulls up the band, The Prodigy/Breathe on her IPod:

> *Psychosomatic, addict, insane*
> *Breathe the pressure...*

'I wish I could say I am lost in my own private thoughts. But the truth is, I woke up today feeling nothing. Nothing. I just want to bask in the nothingness for a while. Is that wrong? It feels so empty and yet, it's offering me comfort, too. No anger. No sadness. Nothing.'

The digital recorder continues recording in case Kristyn decides to speak. For now, there is only the faint sound of music blaring from her earbuds, the soft sound of her lips parting while blowing smoke rings and an occasional serenade from the cricket still hiding in the floor vent.

chapter five

Q. "Tell me what a day in the life of Kristyn Kutter is like at school."

Kristyn's eyes repetitively dart from the window to the door like windshield wipers.

'I could shirk this scene right now. I mean, come on. I don't really feel like recounting another shitty day of my life. But I know you won't let up until I answer. Just remember…you asked for it.'

A. "I get called names."

Q. "Such as?"

A. "Slut, whore, skank and bitch."

Q. "Anything else?"

'Oh, come on. Isn't that enough titillation for you?'

A. "I get shoved and slapped 'bout sometimes."

Q. "Anything else?"
'Do you get pleasure out of hearing 'bout my misery?'

A. "Guys."

Q. "Guys?"

A. "Yeah. They only care 'bout getting off. They don't want my heart, just my fanny."

Q. "How does that make you feel?"

A. "Depressed. Dirty. Lonely."

She then whispers.

A. *"Humiliated."*

And yet, despite feeling depressed, dirty, lonely and worst of all, humiliated, she woke-up in bed today next to a random hook-up she scored MDMA off the night before at a local club. She had to practically drag him out of her bed by his long blonde locks and shove him, with pants, shirt and shoes in hand, out her bedroom window and onto the roof before her mum came in to wake her up for school.

Hours later, she's still struggling to remember the night before.

What the fuck was his name? Tanner? Tank? Tim? Tosser? Oh, well. Guess the shag wasn't memorable, but the MDMA he sold sure was. Hope I see him again — at least for the score.'

chapter six

Q. "Are your parents aware of what you have been going through?"

A. "No."

Q. "Why not?"

A. "Haven't told them."

Q. "Any particular reason why not?"

A. "They wouldn't understand."

Kristyn looks downward at her newly decorated white trainers. Instead of band names and harsh words — this time — she covered the shoes in black ink question marks.

'I question everything 'bout life. Why I'm here? Why mean people exist? Will it ever get better? Am I doomed to be a loser my whole life? I wonder why, after all the shit I've been through. After all the shit they've put me through... why am I still here? What's the point?'

A. "They don't get what it's like to be a loser."
She puts her hand over her mouth, pretending to be shocked.

A. "*Oops*, I mean, a teen, today."

Q. "Do you feel unworthy of being loved by your parents?"

She turns the tables.

A.   "Do you feel unworthy of being loved by *your* parents?"

Q.   "Let's keep the focus on you."

She leans forward and replies in a rather catty tone.

A.   "*You* don't, do *you?*"

Q.   "Are you going to answer my question?"

Kristyn pulls the sleeves down on her shirt enough to cover her hands. It is a mild attempt on her part of hide herself from the world.

'I feel unworthy to be loved by a fucking earthworm. What does that tell you?'

A. "'S hard to live up to their expectations, you know?"

Q.   "Do your parents put demands on you?"

She takes a drink of soda.

A.   "Like what?"

Q.   "Do they expect you to get straight A's?"

A.   "They never really hassle me 'bout anything."

Kristyn shrugs her shoulders and begins pulling her hair.

Q. "Are you feeling anxious?"

A. "Why?"

Q. "I notice you are pulling on your hair."

Kristyn suddenly drops her hand down onto her lap.

A. *"Sorry."*

Q. "It was just an observation. No need to apologize. Getting back to…"

Kristyn suddenly shouts out.

A. *"Argh!"*

Q. "What is wrong?"

'Haven't you ever felt like screaming for no reason?'

A. "Nothing."

Q. "It is obviously something otherwise you would not have shouted out."

'Getting me to confess 'bout it will be like pulling chewing gum out of my hair. Tedious and painful.'

A. "It's just…"
She hesitates.

A. "It's just that…"

'Oh, cut the crap, Kristyn. Say what you mean, girl, before I knock the words out of you with a smack to the back of the head.'

She thinks on the painful release a hit to the head might provide. Or, at the very least, deliver a brief distraction from the extreme pressure she is currently experiencing.

'Oh, God! I can't fucking breathe!'

A. "It's just that the more I share 'bout myself in these, whatever you call them…"

Q. "Sessions."

A. "The more I share, the crazier I feel I am."

Q. "No more than most."

A. "Is your comment supposed to help me feel better?"

Q. "The more you share about yourself, Kristyn, the more you will discover about yourself."

Kristyn wears a tentative smile.

A. *"Great."*

Q. "Self-discovery can be an adventure."

A. "Well in my world, you'll likely stumble upon a snake or two."

Q. "Do snakes frighten you?"

Kristyn releases a sarcastic laugh.

A.   "No. But, I've shagged a few. *Unfortunately.*"

chapter seven

Kristyn enters the room in a huff. She slams her purse down on the table, and pops open a can of soda. Fizz from the soda spills over the side of the can and onto her jeans. She reaches for some Kleenex to wipe up the mess while mumbling to herself.

'Fucking hell! You, stupid cow! Can't do anything right, can you?'

She then swallows a few gulps of the sticky drink before setting the can down beside her purse.

Q. "I see you wrote something new on your shoe."

Kristyn raises her right leg and moves her foot side to side, proudly admiring her new artwork. She has once again written the word, 'Slag' in bold lettering.

A. "It's cool, right?"

'It's so not, you simpleton, and you know it.'

Q. "Why did you vandalize your shoe, again?"

Kristyn shrugs her shoulders.
A. "Felt like it, I guess."

Q. "You guess? Or, you know?"

Kristyn runs her hand through her tangled brown hair.

A. "Maybe something had me feeling a bit tizzy at the time I wrote it."

Q. "What upset you?"

'The fact that I woke up today. Isn't that enough of a reason?'

A. "I don't want to talk 'bout it."

Q. "Why the word *slag?*"

Kristyn glances at the spider plant. Only two green leaves remain on it. The rest are dry and brown.

'Once those leaves vanish, so too will the plant. It will be as if it never existed.'

A. "*Lucky plant.*"

Q. "Why the word, *slag,* Kristyn?"

A. "Why not *slag?*"

Q. "Remind me again what a *slag* is?"

A. "A slut."

Q. "Why did you write it on your shoe again?"
Kristyn says nothing.

Q. "No one forced you to write *slag* on your shoe, right?"

Kristyn's body grows rigid, as anger illuminates from her voice.

A. "*They* did."

Q. "Who are *they*?"

She sarcastically replies.

A. "Tossers, wankers and trolls. *Oh, my!*"

Q. "Sorry. Who?"

A. "Kids at school and online."

'*Asses. Every one of them.*'

Q. "How did *they* force you to write *slag* on your sneaker?"

Kristyn rolls her eyes and shakes her head side to side in disbelief.

'*Don't be such a git. You know what I mean.*'

Q. "How do you justify blaming others for something you chose to do?"

Kristyn draws her bottom lip in and nips it hard enough to invoke pain followed by slight relief. She is struggling to accept responsibility for what she knows down inside she chose to do. To avoid taking it — as is her way - she tries justifying her behavior by placing the blame, instead of owning it.
'*If they didn't harass me 24/7 maybe I would have drawn a cheery flower or something.*'

A. "I never fancied myself to be a *slag* until *they* said so."

'So, I became one. Whether it's to fill a void of loneliness, barter for MDMA, boredom, spite, revenge, to forget…or I'm just feeling horny. Whatever. I do what I want. I do who I want. I don't care. It's just easier to be what they think I am. Least for me it is, anyway.'

More *lies*.

Q. "Regardless of *their* opinion of you, *you* are still the one who chose to vandalize her own shoe."

'Don't you think I know that? Fucking hell!'

She tucks the sneaker under her left thigh.

A. "Whatever."

Q. "What did you think of yourself before the *slag* campaign against you began?"

She puts her face in her hands and moans.

'Oh, for fuck's sake! Let it go already.'

She looks up with a faint expression of disgust.

A. "I thought I was connecting."

Q. "You mean relationships?"

Her foot is beginning to fall asleep. She removes it from underneath her thigh and plants it firmly on the floor.

A. "I didn't realize I was going to be branded sodding, *Hester Prynne* for it."

Q. "Have you ever asked why *they* call you a *slag?*"

'Some people make mistakes. I, on the other hand, have a knack for royally fucking things up.'

A. "Once."

She mumbles.

A. *"Unfortunately."*

Q. "Who did you ask?"

A. "Ian Rhodes."

Q. "Who is Ian Rhodes?"

A. "A complete wanker. He'll do it with anyone or anything. Even a hydrant stands a chance if you put lacy knickers and a short skirt on it."

Kristyn sarcastically laughs.

A. "Ian can put a horny toad to shame."

Q. "You do not think highly of Ian, do you?"

Her eyes grow wide.
'You wouldn't either. Trust me.'

A.   "He's revolting with his baggy pants, shaggy unkempt dirty-blonde hair, warped teeth and this white gunk that's always piled up in the corners of his eyes. All he does is smoke spliff, skate, shag, and sleep in class. Total loser."

Q.   "Why date Ian if he is so repulsive?"

A.   "I didn't date him."

'Blech!'

A.   "It's a pity shag thing. If you can even call it that."

Kristyn shudders, recalling her regrettable encounter with Ian. Both were completely wasted at a party. Him on larger. Her on MDMA. They bumped into one another in the garage. Three wretched thrusts against the rubbish bins beside his mom's shiny black Mercedes, and it was over. Pants up. Skirt patted back down and off they went in separate directions.

Q.   "Why sleep with someone you are not attracted to?"

A.   "Low self-esteem, plus loneliness, plus MDMA, equals a very bad decision I wish could be undone."

'Like I said, I have a knack for royally fucking things up."

Q.   "What was Ian's answer when you asked him why people call you a *slag?*"

A.   "Nothing."

Q.   "Nothing?"
A.   "Well, he did want a shag in the parking lot between English and History."

Kristyn makes retching sounds.

Q.   "Did you shag him?"

A.   "I told him to piss off."

Q.   "Why not shag him this time?"

Kristyn furrows her brows.

A.   "Simple. I was sober."

chapter eight

Q.   "I would like to continue where we left off last session."

'I certainly don't. You're going to talk 'bout that fuckwit Ian Rhodes, again. I can feel it in my bones. I just know I'm right. As if those fifteen seconds in the garage wasn't enough punishment.'

Kristyn applies strawberry scented lip gloss. She returns the lip gloss to a small pocket inside her purse before fumbling around inside the bag for her phone. She gives the phone a quick look, before dropping it back into her purse with a look of disappointment upon her face.

No missed calls.

'I can't say I'm surprised.'

Q.   "We last discussed you being called a *slag.*"

She imagines Ian's wretched lips coming at her neck like a famished vacuum. Slurrrrp!

'Gross!!! Just gross!!! Shut it down, Kristyn. Shut it down!'

She decides to take command of the conversation to avoid discussing her unenchanted encounter with Ian anymore.

A.   "I don't understand why I've got a bad reputation and other girls at my school don't."

Kristyn kicks off her shoes. To date, slag is still the only word written on the right shoe surrounded by a maze of different sized question marks.

A.   "I mean, we all do the same stuff. It's so confusing."

Q.   "Not understanding why, you are being singled out is understandably..."

'It worked! No more talk of knob head Ian.'

A.   "It seems the more I fight back, the worse it gets."

Kristyn runs her hand through her thick brown locks. Her index and middle finger become tangled. She pulls down hard. The strands give way and her fingers are released.

A.   *"Stupid hair."*

Q.   "What about sex?"

She watches as the broken strands of hair leave her hands and float freely down onto the floor, before turning her attention back to sex talk.

A.   "What 'bout it?"

Q.   "What makes one encounter you have with someone different from another?"

A.   "I don't know. Lots of things, I suppose."
She pushes her hair behind her ears.

Q. "What would you call your encounter with Ian?"

A. "A clusterfuck of mass proportions."

Q. "I *see*."

A. "I wish I could *un-see*."

She shudders.

Q. "Have you considered taking things slower?"

A. "I'm not dating sloths."

Q. "I mean, getting to know a person. Maybe date them for a
while before engaging in sex."

A. "No."

Q. "Why not?"

A. "I'm 'bout being in the moment."

Q. "What about love?"

*Kristyn remains silent. Love is a touchy topic. She averts her eyes to the
window. A thunderstorm has arrived, slamming giant raindrops against
the windowpane. For a moment, she fears the glass might shatter. Much
like her heart in the last year.*

Q. "You are aware loose behavior can put you at a greater risk
for STDs?"
A. "*Eh*, so."

Q.   "Having sex with someone is serious."

She replies in a nonchalant manner.

A.   "Spare me the crotch infestation lecture. I've heard."

Kristyn's cell phone suddenly rings. Her heart flutters as she retrieves the phone from her purse.

'Oh, please, oh please let it be…Ugh! Wrong number. Fuck!'

Q.   "That's a nice tune your phone plays when it rings."

A.   "It's from a song from like 2000 or something."

Before being asked, Kristyn puts her phone on vibrate and then drops it back into her purse.

Q.   "What sort of music do you like?"

A.   "Depends on my mood. I like listening to techno when I'm in the mood to dance."

Code for: drop hits of MDMA to dance and try and forget 'bout my shitty life for a while.

A.   "But I really like alternative, industrial, goth, grunge and metal. The grittier, the better. I like songs that reach my soul, not just my ears, you know. I want to feel something. I think that's why I listen to bands who are real. I don't care if they're popular. Their music has to speak to my soul."

Q.   "So, you tend to relate to the songs you hear."

A.   "Pretty much."

Q. "Do you want a boyfriend?"

A. "*Ah.* Can't we keep talking 'bout music?"

Q. "We can discuss music later. Let's continue working on you. Okay?"

Kristyn pouts.

Q. "Are you going to answer my question?"

A. "I told you already. I don't date anymore."

Q. "Why not?"

A. "Ask Jamey Marotto."

She then coughs and speaks at the same time.

A. "Stupid tosser."

Q. "We will get to discussing Jamey soon."

A. "How 'bout *never.*"

Jamey

I'm outside laying on my back in the soft grass right now and staring up at the glittering sky while listening to Mazzy Star, wondering if like the song, 'Let Me Get There' if I ever will find *the groove* again. I'm so fucking lost right now.

I keep listening to the song over and over. The singer's voice hypnotizes my soul while the music brings tears to my eyes. I prefer listening to Mazzy Star - all music for that matter - on vinyl. It just sounds better. At least to me it does. But I can't bring my record player outside. So, I'm listening to it on MP3. Digital always sounds like shit. But what can you do?

I think I might go vinyl shopping this weekend. I've got some money saved up. Okay, that's a lie. I nicked forty-bucks off Ian when he was busy feeling up my bum while giving me a hug. The idiot thought I was feeling him up in return when I was taking the money out of his back pocket. You know what? Screw records. I've had a shit week. I need to dance. I hope I run into that Tanner, Tommy, Tosser - whatever his name is at the club. He'll do me right...and then do me proper. Wink! Wink!

The stars are so bright tonight. Wish I was a star right now. How cool would it be to hang out in the sky twinkling light down on the world? How cool would it be having everyone admire you with kindness? How cool would it be having the worlds eyes on you? How cool would it be to be a part of something like a constellation and feel like you really belong? How cool would it be knowing how bummed people feel when dark clouds hide you from view? Wish I was a star instead of having to wish on one.

Speaking of stars...Mazzy Star "Fade into You" is beginning to play. I think I'll close my eyes and try not to think of Jamey and our countless make outs.... but I know that won't happen. I miss him so much. But then again, FUCK HIM!

chapter nine

Q.   "What is love to you, Kristyn?"

A.   "Overrated."

Q.   "What do you feel when I say the word, *love?*"

Hearing the 'L' word makes me want to puke.'

She says nothing out loud.

Q.   "Do you feel anything?"

She reluctantly replies.

A.   "Emptiness."

'Oh, and revulsion, too.'

Q.   "Why emptiness?"

Kristyn releases a sigh and kicks her right foot out before bringing it back.

She becomes pithy.

A. "Love's a mirage."

Q. "A mirage, *hmm?*"

A. "Pretty much."

Q. "For someone who thinks so little of love, you have some interesting observations about it."

Kristyn looks out the window.

A. "So."

Q. "Why do think love is a mirage?"

She turns her attention back.

A. "Because it eventually leaves you gutted."

She then lights up a cigarette and takes a deep drag.

Q. "Everyone who loves gets hurt, Kristyn."

She scoffs.

A. "Some more than others."

She takes another drag and flicks ash into a soda can.

Q. "Do you love yourself?"

A. "I want to crawl out of my own skin."

Q. "Why do you feel this about yourself?"

She takes another drag.

'If you were me, you'd feel the same way.'

She shrugs her shoulders.

Q. "Would you like to love yourself?"

'No. Way. In. Hell.'

A. "I don't see the point, really."

Q. "Why not?"

A. "I just don't."

Q. "What if I told you, you are already showing love for yourself."

Her eyes narrow, full of suspicion.

A. "How in the fuck am I doing that?"

Q. "By getting to know who you are in these sessions."

She sharply replies.

A. "I already know who I am. *Cheers.*"

Q. "We never truly know who we are or what we can endure until we are put in situations that test us."

A. "Well, I've already failed life's test."

Q. "I want to help you learn to love yourself."

Well, I certainly don't want to love myself. Nor do I want that disgusting 'L' Word anywhere in my life for that matter. EVER!'

A. "Is it true we can think we know someone, but never really know them at all?"

Q. "Sometimes, yes."

A. "Then it's possible I could never really know myself no matter how much…"

She does air-quotations.

A. … *'self-discovery'* I do in these sessions."

Q. "That depends."

A. "On what?"

Q. "Your willingness to drop barriers and override any fear."

She rolls her eyes in disbelief.

A. "Seriously?"

Q. "You do not give yourself enough credit, Kristyn."

A. "And you, give me *way* too much."

i love him. i hate him. i love him. i i love him. i hate him. i love him. i hate him. i love him. i hate him. i love him. i hate him. i love him. i hate him. i love him. i hate him.

i love him. i hate him. i love him. i hate him. i love him. i hate him. i love him. i hate him. i love him. i hate him. i love him. i hate him. i love him. i hate him. i love him. i hate him. i love him. i hate him. i love him. i hate him. i love him. shit!

Jamey Marotto

is a total

HEADFUCK!!!

Jamey had called me last night and then ignored me the following day at school. He acted as if we never spoke 'bout our feelings for each other or nothing. Tosser! I was so pissed 'bout it that I snuck into a loo stall and wrote a warning to other girls. No. Wait. That's bullshit. I did it to help keep girls away from him. I don't think my heart can take it right now. Why is he headfucking me? More importantly…why am I letting him?'

chapter ten

Q.   "You are stronger than I think you realize."

Kristyn remains silent and maintains a stoic posture.

'You are too easy to fool. Too, easy.'

Q.   "You disagree?"

She rolls up the right sleeve of her black burned out shirt, exposing numerous cuts.

A.   "Exhibit A happens to disagree with you."

Kristyn's arm and wrists bear signs of the battle she has been fighting within herself. Her numerous scars are now on display like war wounds unworthy of the valor of a purple heart.

'I'm pathetic, not brave.'

Sprinkled between the old cuts are a few fresh ones etched as recent as yesterday. She stares down at her scars, remembering how and why each one came to be.

'So many not-so-fond- memories to recall. Where do I begin?'

Q. "Pull your sleeve back down, please."

Kristyn wears a puzzled expression upon her face.

A. "Why? I thought you were going to help me sort out this cutting thing I do."

Kristyn half-heartedly pulls the shirt sleeve back down.

Q. "I would like to revisit your old shoes, today."

'For fuck's sake. Let it go already.'

A. "Why?"

Q. "Because you chose to wear them today and I would like to discuss why."

Kristyn folds her arms in defiance.

'Well I don't feel like talking 'bout my shoes.'

Q. "Please read some of the words out loud."

She thrusts her right sneaker forward.

A. "Read them yourself."

Q. "No. You do it."

She knows which words are meant to be heard, but deliberately reads the band names out loud instead.

A.   "Prodigy. The Cure. Incubus. Slipknot. Disturbed.'

Q.   "The words, Kristyn."

She sighs loudly.

'Gawd! You can be so annoying!'

A.   "Fine. Slag, whore, easy, loser, stupid, fat, dumb, lame, dork, geek, pathetic, nobody, nothing, zero and worthless."

Q.   "Do you believe those words apply to you?"

A.   "Wouldn't have written them otherwise."

Q.   "Why did you choose to wear those shoes today?"

A.   "Do I need a reason to wear shoes? I mean, besides avoiding bacteria or getting worms."

Q.   "For those particular shoes, yes, you do need a reason."

A.   "*They* think the words apply to me. I happen to agree."

'Yesterday was a shit day at school for me. I don't want to talk 'bout it because you'll just dissect the hell out of like a damn frog pickled in formaldehyde.'

Here's what happened:

The bullying got so bad; I spent my lunch hour hiding out in the bathroom, cutting on my arm and secretly crying. Fearlessqueenofmean, who doesn't even go to my school, spread a rumor 'bout me shagging some cheerleader's boyfriend. I don't even know the guy. Or the cheerleader. But that didn't matter. Apparently. I personally think she's the one who's been shagging the guy. The cheerleader was 'bout to find out. So, she threw the blame my way to avoid getting her own ass kicked.'

'I chose to wear the shoes because I was hoping if I showed I agreed with the names they were calling me, they would leave me alone. Didn't work — unfortunately.'

Q.   "When you say, *they*, you mean the bullies?"

She mumbles.

A.   *"Who else."*

Q.   "How do you feel about getting rid of the shoes?"

She perks up. Shocked.

A.   "Have you gone mad?"

She thrusts both sneakered feet forward for emphasis.

A.   "*Hello!* Converse. Do you have any idea how much these shoes cost?"

'You really are clueless, aren't you?'

Q.   "They cannot be worth much if you wrote on them with a permanent marker."

A.   "I was making a point."

Q.   "Looks more like a cry for help to me."
She snaps back, emphatically over-annunciating each letter.

A.   "P.O.I.N.T. Point."

'I may repeat mistakes, but never points.'

Q.   "Do you not think your self-worth is more valuable than a pair of vandalized sneakers?"

Kristyn sneers.

A.   "I didn't vandalize them."

Q.   "Then what do you call what you did to your shoes then?"

A.   "Enhancement."

Q.   "You can do what you wish with the sneakers."

Her eyes grow wide.

A.   *"Really?"*

Q.   "I recommend throwing them out."

'Of course, you would recommend the rubbish bin.'

She glances down at the shoes.

A.   "But I don't have to toss them if I don't want to, right?"

Q.   "Correct."

A.   "It's my choice to keep the shoes if I want, right?"
Q.   "You seem surprised."

A. "I am. My choices never mattered before now."

Q. "Your choices have always mattered."

A. *"Pssh."*

The only choices of mine that have mattered are the endless string of bad ones I keep making. Shagging Ian Rhodes for example. Bad…very bad choice'

Q. "You have had the power of choice all along, Kristyn."

Her body grows rigid.

A. *"Wait.* Are you saying I'm responsible for stuff that's happened to me because of my choices?"

Q. "Some of it. *Yes.*"

Kristyn shoots a quick look down at the sneakers.

Q. "What do you think will happen if you take a step towards living a more positive life?"

'Same thing that always happens.'

A. "Nothing."

Q. "Throwing the sneakers away would be a good start."

A. "What if I toss them and nothing changes. Then what?"

Q. "What if everything changes and for the better?"

A.   "Fine."

'You better be right 'bout this. These are Converse I'm putting in the rubbish bin. Converse!'

She then gets up from the chair, shuffles over to the trashcan and drops the shoes in, before shuffling back and plopping down into the chair.

Q.   "Throwing those shoes away was a necessary step for your recovery, Kristyn."

A.   "I'll remember that when I'm walking out of here in my bare feet."

'I just hope I don't contract strongyloidiasis or some other batshit sounding disease, I can't pronounce proper or hardly spell.'

chapter eleven

Q. "You seriously have a tattoo?"

Kristyn flashes a Cheshire smile.

A. "*Nope,* but, if I did, it would be a butterfly."

Q. "Why a butterfly?"

A. "Because a caterpillar is this gnarly looking creature. No one wants it around. So, eventually, it locks itself inside darkness. You know, a cocoon, where it is hidden away from the rest of the world for a while."

Q. "Do you relate to the caterpillar?"

A. "Yes. It lives in isolation. Then, when it's ready, it emerges from the darkness, back into the light. Only now, it is a new creature. Something beautiful and acceptable to the world. A butterfly."

Q. "Is that how you feel after reemerging from one of your dark moods?"

A. "Sometimes. But I always become a caterpillar, again."

Kristyn's eyes brim with tears.

'Stop weeping before your mascara runs down to your kneecaps.'

She quickly switches the topic.

A. "I do have some piercings."

Q. "Why piercings and not tattoos?"

A. "Piercings are easier to erase if you get tired of them."

Q. "What about the scars from cutting?"

Kristyn glances down at her wrists.

A. "What 'bout them?"

Q. "They are not so easy to erase, yet you continue making new ones."

A. "What the fuck's that got to do with anything? My scars are different than tattoos or piercings."

Q. "How?"

'You just can't leave it be, can you?'

A. "They bring me comfort."

Q. "Comfort? Or, conflict?"

A. "There's no conflict. I like having them. I choose to have them."

Q. "Do you like remembering painful events in your life?"

'I can't deal with the pressure you're putting on me. I just can't.'

A.   "I'm done chatting."

Q.   "Okay. But know your choice will delay your progress."

'Ha! I won!'

She spends the evening cutting while at the same time, trying to convince herself today's session was a victory for her because she called the shots and ended it. Truth is, she never felt more like a failure for quitting when things got a little bit tough to handle.

chapter twelve

Q. "Are you called any other names besides the ones we have already discussed?"

A. "More than a dictionary can hold."

Q. "Such as?"

Kristyn clicks her tongue several times while thinking.

A. "*Oh!* Kutter. *They* love to call me, Kutter."

Q. "Your last name?"

A. "Ironic, isn't it?"

Q. "In what way?"

A. "My mum says, *'you become what you say'.*"

Q. "Am I missing something?"

Kristyn carefully slips her left index finger under the cuff of her shirt and caresses her right wrist. A feeling of pleasure washes over her.

A. "Don't you get it? I'm a cutter and my last name is Kutter."

Q.   "*Oh*, now I understand."

A.   "It's a brilliant coincidence, *no?*"

Q.   "No."

She cranes her neck back. Surprised.

A: "*No?* Why not?"

Q.   "I thought no one knew you self-harmed, or did I misunderstand?"

A.   "*They* don't. It's why I fancy being called Kutter. It's like I'm putting one over on *them* only *they* don't know it."

Kristyn puts both legs out in front of her and crosses her right foot over her left and chuckles.

Q.   "I find it rather sad and disappointing."

A.   "What? Why?"

Q.   "How you see your last name in that way. You have so much potential Kristyn and yet, you continually choose to sluff off serious issues instead of dealing with them."

'Ugh! Make up your bloody mind, will you.'

A.   "I thought I was dealing. You even said so."

Q.   "Because I thought you were. Obviously, I was wrong."

A.   "Fucks sake! I don't see anything wrong with what I said."

Q.   "Therein lies your problem."

'My problem? Umm…make it plural, then you've got it right.'

A.   "What problem?"

Q.   "You happen to have the last name Kutter, spelled with a 'K' and not a 'C', as you clearly wish it to be."

She tartly replies.

A.   "And why would I wish that?"

'As if you don't already know the answer, Kristyn. Come on. Who are you trying to fool?'

Q.   "To justify your secret behavior and avoid taking any responsibility for it."

Kristyn hisses.

'Piss off!'

A.   *"Whatever."*

Q.   "Kutter…"

Kristyn cuts in and does sarcastic air-quotations to emphasize her anger.

A.   "With a *'K'* and not a *'C'.*"
Q.   "Kutter is your last name. Nothing more."

A. "That's your opinion."

Q. "No. It is a fact."

A. "Wh*aaaa*teve*rrrr*."

Q. "'*Whatever*', seems to be your stock reply whenever the truth surfaces."

Kristyn bites her bottom lip, then snaps back.

A. "*Wh-aaa-t-ev-errr!*"

Q. "We will get nowhere if you continue replying with '*whatever*'."

A. "Whatever."

Q. "Okay. Let's try something else."

A. "Whatever."

Q. "Enough, Kristyn."

Kristyn opens her mouth to speak, before abruptly shutting it. Although she feels compelled to continue the 'whatever' game, she senses it will cost her extra sessions. Something she desperately wants to avoid.

Q. "Why do you think *they* call you Kutter instead of Kristyn?"

Kristyn shrugs her shoulders.

Q. "Are you certain no one knows of your secret behavior?"

A. "If anyone knew, it wouldn't exactly be *'secret behavior'* now would it?"

Q. "I cannot help but think if you were called Kutter in reference with a *'C'* and not a *'K'* you would somehow feel validated and included by your peers."

She stands up and places both hands on her hips.

A. "Validated? Included?"

Q. "Sit back down, please."

She plops back in the chair like a sack of potatoes.

Q. "Obviously, you disagree."

A. "If anyone found out I'm a cutter, I would feel violated and mortified, not validated or included."

'And for the record, I don't give a crap 'bout validation or inclusion, especially when it comes to dealing with those tossers at my school.'

Lie! She does care.

chapter thirteen

Kristyn avoids making eye contact. She pulls her right leg up and begins tugging at several loose threads on the bottom of her jeans.

A.   "Oh. You'll be happy to know, I'm still a slag."

Q.   "I am not happy to hear you say that about yourself."

Kristyn pulls hard on one of the threads. It breaks free. She then begins rolling it between her left thumb and index finger until it forms a ball.

A.   "I don't get why when I do certain stuff, things always seem to kick off. It's so maddening. But, *whatever.*"

Q.   "What sort of stuff do you mean? I think I have an idea but give me your interpretation."

Kristyn attempts a hint at her meaning, by playfully arching her eyebrows a few times.

A.   "Get it?"

Q.   "Just tell me."

Why don't I just draw you a picture, instead?'

A. "Okay. Let's say I hook up with a guy."

Q. "Hook up?"

A. "Yeah. Mess 'round for a bit. Again, nothing other girls in my school aren't doing, too."

She takes a drink.

A. "Only difference is their reputations aren't being soiled."

Q. "Unlike yours."

A. "Yeah."

Q. "Just so I can clarify, *'hooking up'* means…?"

A. "Making out, shagging and stuff."

Q. "I see."

Kristyn becomes a tad defensive at the tone of the statement.

A. "*Everyone* at my school is doing it. *Everyone.*"

Q. "I highly doubt *everyone* is doing it."

'Did you take a poll to get that particular information?'

A. "*They* are."

Q. "My guess is you only hear about the ones who actually are or the ones who make up rumors about themselves to feel included. You do not hear about the ones who are not doing it."

A. "Why would someone spread a rumor 'bout themselves doing it? That's just dumb."

Q. "Is that how you justify your loose behavior?"

A. "What do you mean?"

Q. "According to you, *everyone* is doing it."

A. "Right."

Q. "Yet, it has earned you a questionable reputation."

Kristyn sneers.

'Judgmental bitch!'

A. "Hook-ups are no biggie."

Q. "Hook-ups are a very big deal."

A. "Why? You have fun and move on. I've even seen it on the telly and in movies. You're making it sound bad, when it's not. Loving someone is so much worse."

Q. "Hooking-up is bad, Kristyn. More than I think you realize."

Kristyn releases a loud sigh.
'Here comes the sodding lecture.'

Q. "Hollywood and real life are not the same thing."

'Well, duh!'

Q. "TV and movies are fantasy, not reality."

Kristyn rolls her eyes.

A. "I know."

She then stares out the window.

'Sure, would be nice though if they were. I would find the perfect guy who would love me and never break my heart. Though, with my luck, some jerk-off Hollywood writer would kill the poor bastard off.'

Q. "Are you promiscuous hoping for peer acceptance?"

She snaps back.

A. "I don't need or want anyone's approval."

'Oh, yes, you do. Stop lying.'

She grows agitated at herself.

'I'll never admit it out loud!'

Q. "Why continue hooking up if it brings you so many problems?"

A. "Maybe I like the attention. Maybe…"
She pauses for emphasis.

A. "… I like *doing* it."

Q. "Are you being honest?"

She answers with a defiant tone.

A. "Yup."

'Hell, no!'

Q. "I do not believe you are being honest with yourself."

She gives a hard glare.

Q. "Unlike television and movies, real life has real consequences. Sometimes we do not understand the consequences of our actions until it is too late."

'I'd almost rather be shagging Ian right now than listening to this shit.'

Q. "I believe your sexual behavior goes beyond trying to fit in with your peers."

A blank stare washes over Kristyn's face.

Q. "It is rather obvious your self-hatred runs deep. You abuse yourself with cutting and other forms of self-harm. You also allow others to use you because you do not love yourself."

Kristyn is starting to suffocate under the weight of the truth presently bearing down on her shoulders.
'I need some fucking air – like RIGHT NOW!!!!!!!'

A. "I'm done talking."

She abruptly stands up and walks out the door.

Session over.

Later that night….

Kristyn stands before the bathroom mirror. She stares at her reflection in disgust. She then spends the next half-hour writing hateful words over her reflection using; lipstick and eyeliner, until the mirror is practically covered.

The next half-hour she spends reading the words over and again, while staring at bits and pieces of her revolting reflection.

The next hour she spends scrubbing the mirror clean, so her mum and dad don't find out what she did.

The hour after that she spends ordering new lipstick and eyeliner online.

'Dad's going go shit bricks when he gets my next credit card bill. Fuck!'

chapter fourteen

Kristyn stares at herself in the bathroom mirror the following day before attending the next session.

'Christ, Kristyn! You still look like shit.'

She gives her hair a nonchalant toss with her fingers, hoping to restore some form of body. No luck.

'Fuck it.'

The genie of truth had been released from the bottle during the last session. Since then, stress has been smothering her like an un-welcomed lover's arms.

'Ian Rhodes comes to mind! Blech!'

She walks over to the toilet and flushes her half-smoked cigarette — but not before taking one final drag.

As the butt swirls down the mysterious hole, Kristyn wishes she could jump in and be carried away, too.

'I am so dreading today. Let's get it over with you dozy cow.'

Q. "I would like to continue discussing the topic of promiscuity. It is where we left off last session."

'*Of course. Pervert.*'

A. "Can't we talk 'bout something else?"

Q. "I want you to ask yourself why you are promiscuous?"

Enter sarcasm.

A. "Okay. *Why are you such a slut bag, Kristyn?*"

She then stands up.

A. "I don't feel like doing this, today."

Q. "Sit down."

She reluctantly plops back into the chair.

A. "What do you want from me? *Huh?*"

Q. "I want you to answer my question."

She says nothing and instead, turns her gaze towards the window where her attention is momentarily distracted by a clump of fluffy clouds floating by in the sky.

Q. "Kristyn?"

She turns her attention back.

A. "I'm not as slutty as you think."
Q. "I am confused. I thought you said you have been…"

She cuts in.

A. "I may have fibbed."

She then holds her right thumb and index finger half an inch apart and whispers.

A. *"Just a smidge."*

'You didn't lie 'bout your bedroom antics, bitch. Why are you lying now? Is it because of your pal, shame?'

Q. "Why would you lie about something like that?"

A. "I don't know."

Q. "You don't know?"

A. "Maybe I don't have a reason. Maybe I just felt like saying it."

Kristyn holds up a pack of cigarettes.

A. "'S like if someone smokes people assume, they'll get cancer. But not everyone who smokes gets cancer."

Q. "Are you worried about getting cancer from smoking?"

A. "We're all going to die at some point, right?"

She snarks.

A. "I'm just speeding things up a bit is all."

She snickers and lights up a cigarette.

Q. "I do not see the humor in your comment, and neither should you."

'You're such a bore.'

A. "Oh, don't go getting your knickers twisted."

Q. "Back to my question."

Kristyn leans forward and speaks in a cunning tone.

A. *"You're rather curious 'bout my sex life, aren't you?"*

Kristyn then playfully wags her right index finger.

A. *"Naughty."*

Q. "Let's stay focused, *hmm.*"

A. "So, what do you want to know? How many guys I've shagged? If I've been with a girl? What?"

Q. "Do you ever worry your risky behavior could cause more than unpleasant rumors?"

A. "Like what?"

Q. "STD's? Pregnancy?"

A. "That's what condoms are for, right?"
Q. "You use protection every single time you have sex?"

'Did I use protection that night in the garage with Ian? I can't remember.

I was utterly fucked up. Obviously since I shagged Ian up against the bins. Am I late? Oh, God, I can't remember the last time I bled. Shit!'

It's been a good while since Kristyn visited the gynecologist for an exam. The thought of potentially being pregnant by Ian is causing her waves of nausea.

A. "Boundaries, choices, responsibilities and consequences. Life sucks."

Q. "Where do you think your responsibility lies, Kristyn?"

'I'm guessing taking too much MDMA that night I had with, Ian. Please show soon, period. If you do, I promise I'll eat a ton of chocolate. I don't care if I get six billion zits. Just show-up. Please. I can't breed the spawn of Ian Rhodes. I just can't.'

A. "Responsibility with what?"

Q. "Sex."

She becomes spiteful.

A. "If you must know, with Seth. Last night."

'Wow! I almost forgot about Seth. Now, his spawn, I wouldn't mind carrying, but I don't want to be pregnant. I want my period. Yes, I want to feel mind-numbing cramps right 'bout now.'

Q. "I'm sorry? Who is, Seth?"

A. "An FWB."

Q. "What is an FWB?"

A.   "Friend with benefits."

'More like a FWGB. A friend with great benefits.'

Q.   "Seth sounds more like a guy you allow to use you. And there is nothing friendly about being used."

A.   "What if I'm using him? Ever think of that?"

Q.   "Either way…"

Pissed about being judged, she cuts-in.'

A.   "I don't see what the big deal is."

Q.   "Remember when we discussed choices?"

She plays coy.

A.   "Vaguely."

Q.   "Choosing to avoid taking responsibility for your part in something is a choice."

Kristyn parrots back.

A.   *"Choice. Choice. Choice."*

Q.   "Is it possible you are a victim in some of your scenarios by choice, Kristyn?"
A.   "Why would I be a victim on purpose? That's twisted."

Q. "Because labeling yourself the victim in situations such as FWB's, is sometimes easier than taking responsibility for having made bad choices."

'For the record, if you saw Seth, you would not say that. Tall, dark and hot as hell.'

Q. "Your risky, rebellious behavior…."

A. "How is my behavior risky and rebellious?"

Q. "The flaunting of negative words on your shoes."

A. "I threw them out."

Q. "Your participation in random sexual acts."

A. "Not the only one doing it."

Q. "Your need to read garbage written about yourself on social media."

A. "Fucks sake. According to your list, I don't do anything right."

3 days later…

Yes!

I need a Tampon!

Period!

Woo-Hoo!

☾✲

chapter fifteen

Q. "We will get nowhere if..."

Kristyn tartly cuts in.

A. "Maybe I want to be nowhere?"

She then throws a bored glance around the room.

A. "Maybe I want to be nowhere with nothing. No friends. No homework. No drama. No feelings. No breath. Nothing."

Q. "Without breath you would no longer exist."

A. "Exactly."

Q. "Do you not want to exist anymore?"

A. "What's the point."

Q. "Your life."

A. "I don't have one."
Q. "Life is what you make of it."

A. "No. Life is what others force you to make of it."

Q. "You feel others have forced you to see your life as nothing?"

Kristyn watches raindrops run down the windowpane.

A. "It doesn't matter. None of this matters. I don't matter."

Q. "Did something happen? Why are you speaking so negatively, today?"

A. "I'm taking responsibility like you told me to do."

Q. "I think you misunderstood."

A. "How?"

Kristyn's spine stiffens in the chair.

Q. "The point of these sessions is for you to discover who you are. I cannot tell you who to be. You have to learn who you are."

She huffs.

'Of course. Why am I not surprised by this information?'

Q. "I think for you; it is more comfortable to stay with what you know then to step out and change your life."

A. "Piss off!"
Q. "Would you jump off a bridge, if everyone else did?"

A. "That's such a lame question."

Q. "But it makes a valid point. So, would you?"

A. "I know some of my choices are bad. I get it. But I can't help it."

Q. "You can help it. You are a smart girl. You know the difference between right and wrong."

A. "I get confused sometimes. Too many thoughts swirl 'round inside my head all at once."

Q. "What sort of thoughts?"

A. "Why am I here? I mean, what's my purpose in life besides pain and rejection? Why don't I fit in? And, why are Little Debbie Oatmeal pies so bad for you, yet, they taste so *ahh-mazing?*"

chapter sixteen

Q. "Is there someone you like or perhaps love?"

Kristyn takes pause. There was…heck, there still is someone she loves. But he broke her heart and continues doing so by headfucking her every chance he gets.

'It's my fault it keeps happening. I can't help that I still love him. Fuck it! Happiness and love are illusions meant for the delusional. I don't believe in either anymore thanks to Jamey. Fuck em' both! And fuck him, too! Asshole!'

To avoid opening the wound in her heart and putting more cuts on her body, Kristyn makes a choice…and lies.

A. "No."

chapter seventeen

Q. "What worries you the most if your parents learn about your self-harming behavior?"

She whispers.

A. *"They'll stop loving me."*

Q. "How do you feel keeping it a secret from your parents?"

She fidgets about in the chair.

A. "Stressed."

'Can you please change the subject? I don't want to talk 'bout my parents. It's uncomfortable.'

Q. "You are trying to protect your parents. Your heart is in the right place, but…"

A. "So, lying to them 's okay? I mean, long as I'm doing it for the right reason."

Q. "The truth is always better."
A. "But you're saying it's okay to lie to my parents because I'm protecting them, right?"

Q. "The truth always finds its way into the light."

She gives herself a face palm.

A. *"Ugh!"*

Q. "You need to consider getting honest, especially with yourself."

A. "What I need is to keep my lies sorted."

Q. "What scares you the most about the truth, Kristyn?"

She takes pause.

A. "Everything."

BLUE :(

The teacher's out sick so we have a sub for English class, today. She's young for a sub. Not like the retired grandma's I usually see. She told us we could choose. To let her teach Ms. Mason's next lesson plan or spend time writing in our journals. Of course, everyone went for the writing assignment. A quick look around the room and I can tell everyone is on social media screwing off. Including the sub. I think I'm the only one journaling. Oh, well. I'm used to being a loner. Whatever.

The only reason I'm writing is because; I don't have anyone to chat with on social media, I'm not in the mood to read negative crap 'bout myself and I currently lack the cash to shop online for more make-up. I think my dad's going to cut up my credit card if he sees another hundred-dollar eyeshadow palette on the bill.

I'm feeling rather shit anyway. It's been raining non-stop since yesterday. Rain makes me feel so fucking depressed. It's like it breathes life into the monster that lives inside of me. The one who makes me do horrible things to myself.

I'm sitting at my desk right now periodically watching lone raindrops hit the windowpane and slide down, out of sight. I wish I could slide out of sight sometimes.

I'm sure there are a lot of people who wish the same. Not for themselves. But for me. Yeah, I feel that hated by others. I'm not sure I can really blame them because the truth is, I hate myself. Maybe even more than they hate me. I wonder if I should take a poll and find out? Hmm....

I'm really missing Maddison a lot lately. There's so much I want to tell her. I mean, I do anyway, when I'm alone in my room and stuff or if I visit her at the cemetery. But she can't ever answer me back. So, it's not really the same. Not like it used to be, anyway. It really sucks. Talking to her now...well, I basically come off like a loon chatting to myself. Then again, I'm the only company I keep nowadays since she left. Since Jamey left. My life sucks. Why am I here, God? Why?

I wish I was smart enough to figure out how to handle bad stuff. I wish I didn't cut. But I'm not that smart. That fact got verified this morning when I went to the bathroom and saw my name and the word *loser* resting side by side on the wall inside a stall.

Once I was alone, I took out my black Sharpie pen and did the best I could to block it out. Afterwards I felt so depressed. So incredibly depressed. Once I knew it was safe, I dealt with my hurt feelings.

My left arm stings so bad every time I move it to reach certain letters on the keyboard. I have to keep my shirt sleeve down so no one sees what I did. I didn't want to cut, I really didn't. But I'm so gutted with bad feelings right now, I had to let some of them out. So, I did.

I don't know what else to say. I really have nothing else to say, I suppose. Besides, my arm is really hurting. I think I'll just sit here and watch the raindrops continue hitting the windowpane and disappear. And while I do, I'll pretend each drop is me disappearing over and again... at least until the bell rings.

Shit! 20 more minutes to go.

chapter eighteen

Q. "Do you ever call yourself negative names?"

A. "Thought we covered this already. *Crikey!* I wrote nasty words on my shoes. Remember?"

'You know, the shoes you made me toss in the rubbish bin. What's funny is that I don't feel any different since throwing them out. How is that possible?'

Q. "I meant do you ever *speak* negative things to yourself about yourself?"

'Constantly.'

A. "I feel better after doing it. That's fucked up, isn't it?"

Q. "Do you think you deserve to speak to yourself like that?"

Kristyn begins to twirl her necklace.

A. 'I never say what I don't mean.'

'Bullshit. You lie so much you don't even know what the truth is anymore.'

Q. "What does self-harming do for you?"

A. "It helps release the bad feelings I have 'bout myself. At least, until the blood stops flowing."

Q. "What happens when the blood stops flowing?"

A. "The bad feelings return. Sometimes worse than before."

She stares down at her scarred-up wrist currently hidden behind a maroon burnout long T shirt featuring an H.R. Pufnstuf caricature she drew and ironed on herself.

'It was one of mum's favorite shows growing up.'

Q. "That's because the bad feelings never left."

Kristyn begins rubbing the temples of her head.

A. "I have the worst headache right now."

She pulls a bottle of aspirin from her purse and swallows two pills.

Q. "I want you to look in the mirror in front of you, on the table."

She scrunches up her face.

Q. "What do you see when you look at yourself in the mirror?"

A. "Disgust."

Q. "Do you ever talk to your reflection?"

'Mirror Mirror on the wall
Who is the biggest slag of them all?

Kristyn Amelia Kutter.'

A. "Sometimes."

Q. "Why do you choose to look at your reflection while speaking negative words over yourself?"

'Self-loathing. I thought you knew that 'bout me already?'

A. "I don't want to just see the pain in my eyes. I want to feel it in my soul, too."

Q. "Does it bring you the same type of relief you achieve when self-harming?"

A. "Not even close."

Q. "What makes them different from one another?"

A. "I don't know. They just are."

Q. "What do you feel when you speak negative things about yourself while staring at your reflection in the mirror?"

A. "Alive."

chapter nineteen

Q. "Have you ever had suicidal thoughts?"

Kristyn stares out the window. Everything is perfectly still. No wind. No waving tree branches. No rain. No birds. No squirrels. Nothing.

She takes a que from nature and remains silent herself.

Q. "You know, people in your situation..."

Kristyn turns away from the window, now wearing a skeptical gaze.

A. "Sorry? My situation?"

Q. "People in deep emotional pain."

'Like the one sitting before you in the dreaded red chair.'

Q. "It is not uncommon for people in emotional pain to entertain thoughts of suicide."

Kristyn attempts to hide her relatable feelings by acting obnoxious.

A. "I'm shocked."
Q. "Feelings of despair can be overwhelming sometimes."

'You can't even comprehend how overwhelming when applied to my life.'

Q. "But not everyone in a state of despair ends their life. Many choose to get help."

Kristyn's mind immediately thinks of Maddison and her heart sinks.

'But some choose to quit.'

Her mood sours.

A.   *"Whatever."*

Q.   "What does *life* mean to you, Kristyn?"

A.   "Rejection 99.9% of the time out of the roughly 30,000 breaths I take in a day."

Q.   "What about the remaining 1%?"

A.   "Sleep, but not really to rest."

Q.   "Why, then?"

A.   "Because sleeping helps me to forget 'bout my shitty life… until I unfortunately wake up to relive the same hell over and again."

chapter twenty

Kristyn is rummaging through her purse.

A.   *"Shit. Where is it?"*

Q.   "What are you looking for?"

A.   "Nothing."

She continues searching and growing more agitated by the minute.

Q.   "I would like to talk about your piercings."

She looks up with a perplexed expression.

A.   "Why does that matter?"

'Finally.'

She holds up a blue lighter before tucking it back into a hidden pocket inside her purse.

Q.   "Given your addiction to self-harm…"

A.   *"Blah! Blah! Blah!"*

Q. "You have an admitted history of deliberately doing things to feel physical pain, *right?*"

A. "So."

Q. "Piercings can cause that level of the pain you seek."

No reply.

Q.   "How many piercings do you currently have, Kristyn?"

A.   "I have five in my left ear, three in the right."

She then lifts her long-sleeved white Zeppelin concert T shirt, revealing faded scars on her pale stomach, along with a turquoise stoned belly ring resting in her belly button.

A.   "My navel."

Kristyn opens her mouth and shows a white topped post sticking through her tongue.

A. "My tongue."

She points to a small silver hoop sticking out of her left eyebrow.

A. "My eyebrow. I want more, but my mum won't allow it. She says I've wasted enough money on it as it is."

Q.   "Did you enjoy getting pierced?"

A. "I did. I enjoyed the pain I felt."
Q.   "I find it rather intriguing."

A.   "What?"

Q.   "How you desire physical pain to avoid feeling emotional pain."

A.   "It's crazy, right?"

chapter twenty-one

Q. "How do you decide where to self-harm on your body?"

She shrugs her shoulders.

A. "I don't. I just do it."

'Should I share more? Ah, fuck it. May as well. You're just going to drag it out of me… eventually.'

A. "You know, sometimes I let a cut become a scar, sometimes not."

Q. "Why do you choose to make deeper cuts sometimes?"

A. "It depends on how upset I feel."

Q. "So, for you, self-harming is also about control, not just a way of releasing emotional pain."

She ponders the newly discovered revelation.

A. *"Maybe. Hmm…"*

Q. "What happens if you change your mind about a scar? Say, you want to get rid of it."

A. "I won't change my mind."

Q.   "How can you be so sure? People change their minds all the time about things."

A.   "Because each scar I made exists for reasons I never want to forget."

Q.   "Why do you choose to deliberately remember painful things in your life? Most people want to forget moments like that."

She plays coy.

A.   "I'm not most people. Or haven't you figured that out, yet?"

chapter twenty-two

Kristyn arrives thirty-minutes late. She was hoping by doing so, the session would be cancelled. Nope. Still enough time to make it happen.

She looks a mess, on the outside. And feels every bit of it internally, as well. Last night's make-up is barely clinging to her oily skin. Her clothes reek of stale cigarettes and a faint scent of beer she accidentally spilled on her jeans. Her normally clean, coconut scented hair is heaped upon the crown of her head in a messy bun. She sprayed it with extra hairspray hoping to kill any lingering aromas from her night with Seth.

'Yup. I had an FWB moment with Seth last night. Big deal. I was lonely. He was available. I snuck out and met him down the street in his car. Cheap beer, cigarettes, a few thrusts and back home I went. No biggie. I got my needs met…sort of. I mean, at least I'm not feeling lonely any-more. So, mission accomplished. Spent most of the next day in bed eating junk food and watching pointless music videos online.'

The statement she just spoke inside her head suddenly becomes unsettling in her soul.

'Oh, who the fuck are you trying to fool, Kristyn? Yourself? Last night wasn't fun. It was shit. You know it was. I mean, Seth was fun. But I don't know what you were hoping to feel afterwards. Maybe not as lonely? Did you really think Seth held the key to making you feel better? Seriously? Was it even worth it? Look at you. You look as shitty as you feel, swimming in a sea of utter disgust for what you did. You don't feel great. You don't feel whole. You feel lonelier than before your pathetic romp with Seth. Okay, so maybe pathetic isn't a word that suites Seth. But what happened…yeah, I'm feeling pretty damn pathetic right 'bout

now.'

She smells her right armpit.

'And I really stink. Girl, you need a hot shower and a proper douche, as soon as this 'Blah-Blah Session' ends.'

The dreaded red chair immediately hugs her body in the most awkward of ways.

'Uncomfortable. Party of one.'

Q. "Have you ever considered people treat you poorly out of jealousy and not hatred, as you assume?"

Kristyn scoffs. She imagines flipping a coin inside her head to determine her mood.

Heads: Act sweet
Tails: Act sour

'Tails! / Act sour it is.'

A. "Mind if I light a cigarette first before you start hitting me with your annoying questions?"

Q. "I'm sorry?"

Kristyn ignores the acknowledgement at her foul mood and lights a half-smoked cigarette. She did not have the stomach to finish it after last night's event.

'I hate beer. Makes me too bloody gassy.'

She releases a sigh.

A.   "What was your question again?"

Q.   "Do you think people treat you poorly out of jealousy and not hatred, as you assume?"

A.   "Jealous of what? Me?"

She appears outwardly surprised.

Internally, she's laughing hysterically at the thought of 'The Posh Ms. Perfects' being jealous of her Thrift Store wardrobe vs. their 'Neiman-mark up' attire.

'I could almost wee my pants at such an absurd notion.'

Q.   "Jealousy of you is not an impossibility. You project an image of someone who is strong and unique."

Kristyn displays a faint expression of confusion.

A.   "Have you looked at me?"

She re-emphasizes.

A.   "I mean, really *looked* at me?"

Q.   "There is more to jealousy than looks, Kristyn."

A.   "I know. I meant, have you looked in my eyes? Because if so, you wouldn't say something like that."

'Strong? Umm-no. Unique? Yeah, I guess I'll give you that.'

She takes a final drag off her cigarette and blows a few smoke rings, before extinguishing it out.

A.   "It helps if you have something people want. Which I don't."

Q.   "You..."

She interrupts.

A.   "Wait. I take that back. I do have something the boys want. My fanny. But – *meh*."

Q.   "There you go again thinking with a victim mentality."

Kristyn rolls her eyes.

A.   *"Whatever."*

Q.   "Why not choose to see yourself as a survivor instead?"

She remains quiet.

'Seriously? A survivor or what? A night of jack rabbit sex with Ian? If I was strong enough, maybe I might give it a go. But I'm not strong. I'm weak. I'm pathetic. I'm nothing. I know it. I am far from being a survivor. Their words still hurt me every day. The day they don't, then maybe I will see myself as a survivor. If only that day would arrive…could arrive. I wish.'

Q.   "May I see the scars on your wrists?"

Kristyn places her wrists up to her chest and holds them tight against her body in a defensive posture.

A. "I tried to show them to you before and you didn't want to see them. Why do you want to see them now?"

She holds her wrists up to her chest even tighter.

Q. "Why are you getting defensive about showing your scars to me, Kristyn?"

Kristyn slowly lowers her arms back down until they come to a rest in her lap.

'I feel so exposed right now. Like I'm naked, in Antarctica, floating alone on a piece of ice having no idea where the hell I'm drifting to. And there's no seal or polar bear in sight to point me in the right direction.'

A. "I've read stories online 'bout what happens when cutters are found out."

Q. "You are not being found out. Your self-harming behavior is a known problem in this room."

A. "Still."

Q. "Where did you read about self-harmers?"

A. "From other cutters online."
Q. "What did you learn?"

'If you want to know 'bout it so much, look it up yourself.'

A. "I already feel like a freak."

Q. "You are not a freak."

A. "Well, for a cutter, being found out makes us feel like even bigger freaks. No one knows 'bout my cutting. Well, except my best mate, Maddison. She knew."

Q. "Anything we discuss here is confidential. No one has to know anything unless you want them to know."

A. "I don't want anyone to know."

She suddenly finds herself leaving the door of possibility cracked open a bit.

A. *"Yet."*

Q. "If that is your wish, so be it."

A. "Why do you want to see my scars now?"

Q. "Because I want YOU to see them."

A. "I do. I put them there for fuck's sake."

Q. "I want YOU to really look at each scar and think about why you made the choice to self-harm."

Kristyn tugs at her right sleeve. She is silent. She shifts her gaze down at the floor.

A. "I told you. Don't you listen? I cut to release pain."

Q. "Nobody can pull you out of the negative place where you are currently at except you. I can help guide you, but only if you want to be guided."

Kristyn looks up with a glare in her eye.

A. "You want to see my badges of no courage? My cries for help? My failed attempts to seek attention, as most would say. Is that what you want to see?"

Q. "No. I want YOU to see it."

Kristyn rears up in her chair. She then leans forward to emphasize her point and her anger.

A. "I haven't forgotten for one bloody second how, when or why any of my scars exist. The scars *they* caused."

Q. "But you were the one who actually brought the scars into existence."

Kristyn folds her arms.

Piss off! You think you know me. You don't know shit! You don't know how I feel. Why I hurt. Who hurt me. Nothing.'

Q. "YOU chose to manage your pain with self-mutilation. YOU. Not *them.* YOU."

A. "Oh, my, bloody, Gawd! Are you being serious right now?"

Q. "I am."
Kristyn stares ahead, fighting hard not to break. She is not ready to let go of her "hard" exterior. But she can feel the pillars of her tough foundation beginning to crack under the pressure being put on her.

A. "Don't you get it? If THEY hadn't done what THEY did to hurt me, I wouldn't have these wretched memorials etched on my skin as a constant reminder of the hell I've been put through."

Q. "I think you need to ask yourself why you allow anyone to have that kind of power and control over you and your emotions?"

Kristyn shakes her head side to side in disagreement.

'I am not taking responsibility for this. Oh, no, I'm not!'

Overwhelmed, all Kristyn can do is cover her ears and scream.

A. *"Arrrrrgh!"*

chapter twenty-three

Kristyn plops down in the chair. She runs her hand through her hair and adjusts her 'Sex Pistols' Burnout T-shirt before it falls off her right shoulder completely.

A.   "I need a cigarette."

Kristyn reaches for the pack and pulls one out.

Q.   "You really should consider quitting."

'You sound like my mum. Just stop. One lecturing bore in my life is enough.'

Kristyn smirks, lights a cigarette, takes a long drag and exhales.

A.   "Not going to happen today. Maybe tomorrow."

She then snickers.

'Pah! I can hardly keep a straight face after saying that.'

Kristyn flicks the blue lighter with her thumb, causing a flame to appear, then disappear a few times before growing bored and tossing it onto the table.

Q.   "Have you tried to avoid crutching when situations become uncomfortable in your life?"

'Have you tried minding your own business and butting the fuck out of mine?'

A.   "What are you going on 'bout now?"

She takes another drag.

Q. "Your use of destructive behavior to deal with uncomfortable situations."

She scowls.

A.   "It's a cigarette, not spliff for fuck's sake."

Q.   "Do you not see what I am talking about?"

She takes another spiteful drag and flashes a cunning smile.

A.   "Nope."

'I get it. But I'm not 'bout to let you know I do.'

Q. "You use self-harming, smoking, sex, drinking and drugs, among other things, to cope with your issues."

A. "So."

Q. "You do not manage issues in a healthy manner, allowing yourself to heal and move forward in a positive direction."

A. "You do realize I'm a teenager, right? I'm supposed to be immature and scattered. It's my rite of passage."

Kristyn takes another drag from the cigarette.

Q. "Self-destructive behavior is a choice, Kristyn, not a rite of passage."

'According to who? You?'

Q. "You can handle your problems without crutching if you choose to do so."

She smirks.

A.   "Fine."

Kristyn takes one more drag and puts the cigarette out.

Epic fail...

An hour later, Kristyn smoked three cigarettes in a row after reading more nasty stuff about herself online.

'At least I tried to quit. That's got to count for something, right? Right?'

chapter twenty-four

A. "When I look at any scar on my body, I instantly go back to the moment it came to exist. Sometimes I'll even make an old scar bleed again."

Q. "Bleed again? What do you mean?"

A. "I cut in the same place again. *Duh!*"

Q. "I meant, what provokes the desire to reopen an old wound?"

A. "I want to reminisce."

Q. "What do you get out of opening an old wound?"

A. "I deserve to hurt and feel that pain again."

Q. "Why do you feel you deserve to feel this way?"

She shrugs her shoulders.

'I just do. I don't know why. I was sort of hoping you would volunteer the answer because I'm too prideful to ask you why I feel that way.'
Q. "Do you have any good memories in your life to focus on?"

A. "The bad memories far outweigh one *possible* good one."

'Notice how I said 'possible'? It's because if I do have one good memory tucked away somewhere — which is unlikely, trust that there is a bad one attached to it somehow. That's just how my life works. Unfortunately.'

Q. "You could choose to focus on a good memory when things in your life get rough, instead of a negative one which clearly drives your self-harming behavior."

Why bother?'

A. *"Meh."*

Kristyn gives her phone a glance before slamming it back down and releasing a hearty sigh. Several new posts have gone up about her and Ian.

'I can't believe that jerk ran his mouth 'bout that night in his garage! Loser! Why would he do that? Oh, maybe he found out I nicked that money off him and bought some MDMA for myself. I needed it more. Fuck him! His blabbering lips just gave me the excuse I need to stop shagging him — not that I needed an excuse to stop. He was what I consider a 'pity-fuck'. A pity he's who I had available to fuck. A pity he even considers me shag worthy.'

She shakes her head in disgust. But much to her surprise, the disgust she is feeling is aimed more at herself than at Ian.

'Slut. Whore. Skank. Slag. Once again, another noted fuck-up notch to add to your belt. Brilliant, as always, Kristyn.'

Q. "It is your choice which option you want to focus on. The negative or the positive."

'There is no escaping this choice crap, is there? But how do I know which choice to make? How do I know the choice I make is the right one? I mean, I'm the queen of royally fucking my life up. I really wish I had some spliff to mellow my brain out right now.'

All she can do is listen with her head cradled in her hands.

Q.   "Everything in life revolves around choice."

'Wish I had chosen not to shag Ian. Now that would have been a smart choice. But it's too late.'

chapter twenty-five

Q. "I would like to focus on another issue, today."

'I suppose I don't have a say on the topic, huh?'

Q. "I would like to discuss your best friend Maddison."

Kristyn immediately puts her hand up and takes control of the session.

A. "I'm not ready to talk 'bout Maddison, yet. Pick another topic or I'm leaving."

She stands up.

Q. "Okay. We can talk about something else, today. But we are eventually going to discuss what happened to Maddison."

Kristyn sits back down in silence.

Q. "Where have you self-harmed on your body?"

'My body resembles a roadmap to hell. I don't' know where to begin.'

A. "On the inside of my thighs, both of my upper arms, my stomach and hips. You already know 'bout my wrists."

Q. "Do you feel comfortable sharing how your scars came to exist?"

'I would rather drive rusty nails up my toenails then share.'

A. "Nope."

Q. "The places you mentioned where you self-harmed; thighs, hips, stomach and upper arms."

A. *"Uh-huh."*

Kristyn takes a sip of soda before setting the can back onto the table.

Q. "Why those areas?"

A. "Isn't it obvious?"

Q. "No. That is why I asked you."

A. "I don't want to get caught."

She then smirks.

A. "Satisfied?"

Q. "What about your wrists?"

Kristyn gazes down at her exposed wrists and once again falls under the spell of denial.

'Why am I the one feeling ashamed about my scars? They did this to me. I didn't do this to me. They did it.'

She looks up with a blank stare in her eyes.

Q. "You say you do not want to be caught self-harming, yet, you have scars on your wrists. Those scars on your wrists can easily be seen."

A. "Not if I keep them covered up. Which I do."

She then shoots a cunning smile.

Q.   "Did you cut on your wrists for attention, Kristyn?"

Kristyn imitates a game show buzzer.

A.   "*Ehhhh!*"

Q.   "Was it a cry for help?"

A.   "*Ehhhh!*"

Q.   "Were you trying to commit suicide?"

A.   "*Ehhhh!* None of the above, but thanks for playing."

Q.   "Then, why did you do it?"

A.   "I don't know. Why doesn't butter come from butterflies instead of cows? Can you answer me that?"

Q.   "Why are you avoiding answering my question?"

She shrugs her shoulders.

'Because it's none of your business.'

Q.   "When are you going to be serious about getting better?"

A.   "I'm here, aren't I?"

Q.   "You are not giving up much."

She winks.

A.   "The blokes I've shagged will tell you otherwise."

Q.   "I mean information, not sex. I am beginning to think you enjoy playing games because it gives you some control in your life."

'I'm done. You want to think I'm playing games, go ahead. I'm also a mime now, too. Watch me not say shit to you for the remaining time.'

Kristyn lights up a cigarette and tosses the lighter on top of a book on the table. She gets up and walks over to the window. She sees a black crow sitting on a tree branch. She takes a drag and blows smoke at the window. The smoke blows back in her face. She coughs and waves it away. The motion of her hand frightens the crow. He flies away. She stares at the now empty branch until her cigarette is finished and the session time is up.

I Don't Like What I See

Most of the time I'd rather be anyone other than me
When I look at myself in the mirror, I don't like what I see

A stupid worthless loser bitch I never longed to be
Fat thighs, bloated belly, ugly face and knobby knees.

I try so hard to have a life, but bad things continue
to get in my way
I find myself seeking help nightly as I kneel down and
try to pray
But nothing ever changes, my world still remains dark
and grey
Sometimes I wish someone would just put their
arms around me,
and tell me... "It's going to be okay".

chapter twenty-six

The sessions were put on hold for a week because Kristyn was stricken

with the flu.

Q. "Feeling better?"

Kristyn shrugs her shoulders.

A. "I guess. Having the flu sucks."

She coughs.

The congested sound is a lingering reminder of her week from hell.

'At least it got me out of school for a bit. Jamey called a few times. We talked. He said if I wasn't so sick, he would come over after my mum and dad went to sleep. I wanted so much to believe him. But part of me knew, it was more of his headfucking games. Why can't I just put a stop to it? What is wrong with me? I'm kind of glad I was too sick this time to cut. Wow…that's odd.'

Q. "Do you recall where we left off last session?"

Kristyn holds up her scarred wrists.

Q. "That's right. Your wrists. Thank you."

She then rests her arms on her lap.

Q. "Why did you choose to self-harm on your wrists?"

A. "Why not?"

Q. "I thought you wanted to keep your self-harming a secret?"

She remains silent.

Q. "Are you feeling well enough to do this today? Maybe we should reschedule."

She looks up.

'No! I've lost enough time as it is.'

A. "I first cut on my wrists because of a wanker. I wasn't thinking clearly at the time when I did it. Not that I ever do."

Q. "Who is this person you are talking about?"

A. "Just a guy I know. Or knew. *Whatever.*"

Kristyn folds her arms and slouches.

Q. "Just a guy?"

Kristyn looks away.

'Please don't make me talk 'bout him. If I do, I'll start missing him all over again. I don't want to miss him. I hate him. But I still love him. I think. I don't know. My stupid heart. I wish I could get a heart transplant or a lobotomy for my brain so I could forget 'bout him.'

She begins to reluctantly release information about the boy who broke her heart.

A. "He was my boyfriend. Now ex-boyfriend. I've mentioned his name before."

Kristyn then rolls her eyes and whispers.

A.   *"Tosser."*

Q.   "What is his name?"

She snaps back.

A.   "Jamey."

Pain clouds her eyes just hearing her voice speak his name out loud.

Q.   "What happened with Jamey that made you choose to self-harm on your wrists?"

A.   "He was a cheat and every word that came out of his mouth was a fucking lie."

Q.   "Were you hoping to get his attention by self-harming?"

A.   *"Whatever."*

Q.   "Is that a 'yes'?"
A.   "No. It's a *'whatever'*."

Q.   "I'll take that as a *'yes'*."

A.   "Take it any way you want. I don't give a shit."

Q.   "Were you trying to end your life because of Jamey?"

Kristyn is insulted by the suggestion.

*No asshole is worth ending my life over! Especially a lying, cheat like him.
I hate you Jamey. Every bone and organ in my body hates you — except my*

heart. I wish I could evict you from it… but I can't. My fucking heart won't let me. Piece of shit!'

A. "Look. I'm no bleeding Juliet and he's no sodding Romeo. Our relationship was far from being Shakespearian. He gave me a bracelet on our anniversary and then broke-up with me, like two days later. Nice, *huh?*"

Q. "The thick loom beaded bracelet I see on your arm?"

Kristyn grows silent, having drifted off into a moment of happiness when Jamey gave her the bracelet, along with promises of forever. She recalls their endless backseat make-out sessions as 'The Cure' played in the background. The smell of his cologne, as her nose playfully nuzzled his neck. The softness of his shaggy brown hair laced between her fingers. It was a young lover's fantasy. One full of hope and promise. Unlike the reality of what she feels now. Alone. She has since tried recapturing that tummy-flip feeling with nameless, faceless others. But has only found herself falling deeper into loneliness and further away from feelings of love for anyone – especially herself.

A. *"Yeah."*
Q. "The turquoise and purple colors are very pretty."

A. "Purple's my favorite color. He knew that 'bout me."

Q. "Why wear the bracelet if you and Jamey are over?"

'Because I hate him, but I still love him. I want him gone, but I want him nearby. I don't miss him…but I do.'

Q. "Do you use the bracelet as a trigger to self-harm?"

Kristyn shrugs her shoulders.

'Maybe.'

Kristyn gently strokes the bracelet, tending to the painful emotions hidden inside the scars Jamey gave to her the day he first shattered her heart. Since then, he has continued screwing with her heart, emotions and sometimes, her fanny. She has the scars inside and out to prove it.

Q. "Do you miss Jamey?"

'Everyday.'

A. "I wish he never existed."

Q. "Why?"

Kristyn points to her heart.

A. "Because he's still in here."

Q. "Most want to remove themselves from reminders of painful situations and from the people who hurt them. But you don't. Why do you suppose that is?"

Kristyn shrugs her shoulders.

Q. "Why did Jamey break-up with you?"

'Did you miss the part where I said earlier, he was a cheat?'

A. "He just said we were done and walked away."

Kristyn puts her head in her hands and fights the urge to cry.

'I hope I can ask this next question without losing it — entirely. I need help. I can't keep feeling this way. It's killing me.'

She looks up.

A.   "How do I get my heart to STFU 'bout him?"

Q.   "Time."

She mutters.

A.   *"It's been a long time already."*

Q.   "Why do you still wear the bracelet?"

'You already know the answer.'

A.   "To help hide the scars on my wrists."

Kristyn begins spinning the bracelet slowly around her wrist.

Q.   "Maybe it would be a good idea to stop wearing the bracelet since it is a trigger for you. What are your thoughts about that?"

A.   *"Umm…No!"*

Q.   "Why not?"

A.   "Because it helps hide some of my scars. It's funny."

Q.   "What's funny?"

A.   "How I use the bracelet Jamey gave me out of *'love'* to hide what he makes me do out of *'pain'.*"

Q. "Jamey never made you choose to self-harm. You made that choice."

Kristyn scoffs.

Q. "How did you hide your other scars from Jamey during your relationship?

A. "You can hide anything if you want to bad enough."

Q. "Does Jamey know how bad he hurt you?"

A. "Don't know. Don't care to know, either."

'Liar! Liar! Liar! Okay so maybe I don't know. But I definitely do care.'

Dear Jamey,

You're such a twatwaffle! I hate you! I wish I had never met you! Go fuck yourself! You're dumped! My fanny is toooooo good for you!

I left that note in Jamey's locker after he shagged me for a week straight and then ignored me, again! I can't stand his stupid games. Why is he doing this to me? My heart is such a stupid piece of shit for believing anything he says. All he does is talk bollocks. Get it through your head Kristyn! He's a twatwaffle! Remember it!

Jamey dropped my note back into my locker with this:

Dear Kristyn,
Sorry. wanna meet up tonight?

Annnnnnd…..my idiotic heart overrode my brain. I waited up all night for Jamey to tap on my window. He never showed and he ignored my text messages.

'Thanks for headfucking me, AGAIN, Jamey. I wound up spending the evening in my closet with the other monster, instead.'

chapter twenty-seven

Q.   "Did you cut last night?"

Kristyn pulls her right sleeve down and then attempts to lie.

A.   "N-no."

Q.   "I see you have new cuts on your wrist."

'You weren't supposed to see them.'

Q.   "Did our conversation about Jamey cause you to cut?"

Tears well up in Kristyn's eyes.

'Stop. Please. I can't handle any Jamey talk today.'

A.   "I don't want to talk 'bout, Jamey."

As a means of distraction, Kristyn slams her freshly cut wrist down onto her thigh hard and winces. Her frown becomes a slight smile, as a rush of endorphins from the painful hit washes over her. A perfect release.

'Tears – sorted.'

Q.   "Are the new cuts on your wrist because of Jamey?"

A.   "He's not the only reason, you know.

Q.   "What else got you upset enough to self-arm?"

'Jamey. Jamey. Jamey. Oh, yeah. Jamey.'

A.   "The fact I still exist."

Q.   "Why is your existence causing you to self-harm?"

A.   "Look at my life. What I've been put through. You'd feel the same way if you were in my shoes."

Q. "While your response…"

She cuts in with a tone of displeasure.

A. "I'm not a cyborg. I'm a person with real feelings that everyone seems to keep forgetting I have."

'Unbelievable.'

Q. "You need to learn how to better handle issues in your life without harming yourself."

She gives a nonchalant shoulder shrug.

A. "Why mess with a good thing?"

Q. "Inflicting physical pain to relieve yourself of emotional pain is not healthy behavior."

A. "That's your opinion."

Q. "What word comes to mind when you think of yourself, right now, in this moment?"

A. "Broken."

'Like a bird with two wrecked wings who will never get off the ground again, forever stuck pecking shit with the chickens.'

JAMEY </3

When the mind wants to forget, but the heart won't let go.
Blah!
Stupid! Fucking! Heart!
I wish you and Jamey would both PISS OFF!!!!!

chapter twenty-eight

Q. "How long have you been self-harming, Kristyn?"

A. "I don't know. I just started doing it one day and never stopped."

Q.   "Do you remember your first cut?"

Kristyn avoids eye contact.

Q.   "I am not trying to pry. I am trying to help you."

Kristyn quickly snaps back.

A.   "Maybe. I. Don't. Want. Your. Help."

She then scratches an itch on the back of her right calf.

Q.   "How did you connect self-harming with relieving emotional pain?"

A.   "How does anyone connect anything?"

Q.   "Please, answer my question."

A.   "A friend."

Q.   "Who?"

Kristyn looks down at her feet and mumbles.

A.   *"Maddison."*

Q.   "Did Maddison show you how to self-harm?"

A.   "Kind of."

Q.   "What do you mean, *'kind of.'*"

A. "I saw her scars one time, you know, by accident."

Q. "How did that happen?"

A. "We were changing into our PJ's during a sleepover. I saw them on her stomach when she lifted her arms up over her head while taking off her shirt."

Q. "Did Maddison ever tell you about her scars?"

A. "She said they were from surgeries when she was younger."

Q. "Did you believe her?"

A. "I did at the time."

Q. "Did Maddison eventually tell you the truth about her scars or did you ask her?"

A. "She told me."
Q. "What did she tell you?"

A. "She said she cut herself on purpose because it helped her deal with the pain she was feeling on the inside."

Q. "Why do you suppose Maddison told you the truth?"

A. "I don't know. I guess she trusted me to keep her secret."

Q. "How did you feel learning Maddison self-harmed?"

A. "I didn't really know how to feel."

Q.   "You never thought about self-harming prior to discovering Maddison's scars?"

A.   "No. The sight of blood usually makes me want to vomit. But it doesn't seem to bother me when I cut. Don't know why. Just doesn't. Thankfully."

Q.   "What did you say to Maddison after she shared her self-harming secret?"

A.   "Nothing. I just listened."

Q.   "Did you ask Maddison to teach you how to self-harm?"

Kristyn averts her eyes and whispers.

A.   *"Yeah."*

Q.   "Why?"

A.   "I wanted my fucked-up emotions gone, too. Cutting seemed to help Maddison. I wanted the same relief."

Q.   "You must have realized at one point that self-harming does not really work. The pain always returns because it never left to begin with."

A.   *"Yeah,* I know. But it's hard to quit."

Q.   "There are no *'quick fixes'* in bad situations. Only band-aids that eventually fall off, exposing our wounds to the world that will never heal if we do not get to the root of the issue. Self-harming is a band-aid, not a solution."

Kristyn sighs loudly.

A.   "*Brilliant.* I'm fucking up, yet, again."

Q.   "I am not criticizing you or your choices."

A.   "Sounds like you are."

Q.   "I am trying to help you deal with your issues in a healthier way."

'According to you, I can't deal. And, I don't learn from my mistakes, either — so...'

Q.   "Were you and Maddison together the first time you cut?"

A.   "No. I was alone...*as usual.*"

Kristyn takes a sip of soda.

A.   "Cutting was something Maddison and I did in private. We never really talked 'bout it."

Q.   "What happened that pushed you to self-harm for the first time?"

Kristyn remains silent.

Q.   "Was it your break-up with Jamey?"

Kristyn's palms begin to sweat. She wipes them on her jeans, to hide her nervousness.

A.   "It's complicated."

Q. "How is it complicated?"

A. "Just is."

Q. "Try and explain it to me."

A. "It was a combination of everything going on in my life at the time. I had just started high school at the time. I felt even more overwhelmed. It's like I had all this self-hate and rejection bottled up inside of me over the years, and I had finally found a way to let it out."

Q. "Where did you cut on yourself for the first time?"

Kristyn throws a glance down at her right leg and then looks back up.

A. "My blubbery, inner right thigh."

Q. "Any particular reason why you chose your thigh?"
A. "It's fat and nasty!"

Q. "You are not fat, Kristyn."

'Whatever!'

A. "Nobody would see the scar. But I knew it was there."

Q. "How did it feel keeping that secret for the first time?"

A. "Free."

chapter twenty-nine

Kristyn stares down at her phone, fighting the urge to cry. Today is Monday. But not just any Monday. It is the third Monday of the month — aka: 'Mocha Monday'. The traditional Monday when her and Maddison would

stand in line at the coffee shop for Chocolate Mochas after school. She had stopped and purchased a Mocha Coffee before the session.

'Damn!'

She struggles to swallow a gulp of coffee she just took. The barista sprinkled on too much cinnamon.

'Blech! It's fucking bitter!'

She resumes staring down at her phone.

Q. "Are you reading more nasty posts about yourself?"

She doesn't look up.

A. "No. I'm looking at a picture of Maddison and me being cheeky."

Q. "Cheeky, how?"

A. "We put whipped cream on the tip of our noses after getting our Mochas, then took the pic. We used to get Mocha's every third Monday of the month."

Q. "May I see the picture?"

Kristyn turns the phone around for a quick view.

A. "I snapped it a week before she died."

Q. "Tell me about Maddison."

Kristyn remains fixated on the picture.

'I can't. Leave it alone. Please.'

Q. "It is time we talk about her, Kristyn."

Kristyn puts her cell phone down beside her with attitude.

'First, Jamey. Now, Maddison. I feel like I'm in the middle of a bad nightmare I can't wake myself out of.'

A. "She's gone. What's the point?"

Q. "The impact her loss has had on your life is huge."

'I have no one to share my secrets with now. No one who gets me like you did, Maddison. Why did you have to leave me, Maddison? Why? You're such a selfish bitch! And, this Mocha really tastes like shit.'

Q. "I do not think you realize how much her death has affected you."

'Oh, I am very aware of it! I may come off like an idiot with the choices I make, but I'm not an actual idiot. I'm taking college courses while still in high school for fucks sake.'

Kristyn stares out the window.

Q. "Do you feel like Maddison abandoned you?"

Kristyn lights up a cigarette. She takes a deep drag and exhales.

A. "This topic is annoying me."

I'm also annoyed the barista screwed-up my Mocha. I mean, seriously.

How hard is it to make a fucking Mocha? It's not like you don't make them all day long for other people. Maybe she did it on purpose. Hmm, I wonder if she goes to my school?

Kristyn gets up and walks over to the window. To an outsider, she appears to be looking at the tree. But, in truth, she is staring at her own gloomy reflection in the windowpane staring back at her.

Q. "What happened to Maddison?"

She takes another drag off her cigarette.

A. "You already know."

Q. "Are you afraid to talk about it?"

She does not respond.

Q. "Kristyn?"

She takes another deep drag off her cigarette and returns to the uncomfortable red chair.

A. "Maddison died because of me."

Q. "Why do you blame yourself for Maddison's death?"

Kristyn pulls her knees up to her chest as if seeking some form of self-reassurance. She takes another drag off her cigarette.

A. "Maddison and I were a lot alike, yet we looked nothing alike. We were like those twins…"

Kristyn struggles to find the right word.

Q. "Fraternal twins."

A. "Yeah! Only Maddison was taller than me. She had shiny black hair, unlike this dark-brown stringy mess on my head. And her blue-green eyes were like a never-ending ocean. She was so beautiful inside and out."

Kristen sighs and takes another drag.

Kristyn begins to feel more relaxed as her attention is now focusing on remembering positive things about her beloved best friend.

A. "We both loved horseback riding, writing poetry and designing clothes. Sometimes Maddison's mum took us to Goodwill stores or garage sales where Maddison and I would buy the ugliest clothes and turn them into fun, creative outfits. We used to dream about being on a fashion reality TV show and opening our own clothing boutique."

Q. "So, you both had plans for the future."

A. "I thought we did."

Kristyn takes another drag.

A. "One thing 'bout Maddison that really bothered her, were her big boobs."

Q. "She felt more mature than the other girls in your class?"

A. "She despised all the attention her big boobs drew."

Q. "What sort of attention?"

A. "She had guys always asking her to send pictures of her boobs to their phones. You know, sexting."

Q. "Oh."

A. "I guess the girls at school were jealous of the attention she got. Too bad they didn't realize how much she hated it."

Q. "Did Maddison ever sext any of the boys?"

A. "No bloody way."

Q. "What about you?"

Kristyn stares down at her AA cup breasts and half-smirks.

A. "Are you seriously asking me that?"

Kristyn licks her dried lips.
A. "I blame myself for most of what Maddison went through in the last year of her life."

Q. "Why do you blame yourself?"

Kristyn half-heartedly shrugs her shoulders.

A. "Guilt by association."

Q. "What do you mean, '*guilt by association*'?"

A. "Maddison wasn't bullied much, until she stuck up for me against Claire."

Q. "How did Maddison defend you against, Claire?"

A. "She told the queen of the *Posh Miss Perfects*, Claire, to *'fuck off'*. After that, her life was hell."

Q. "You know, Maddison's death was not your fault."

Kristyn slides the palm of her hand up and down on her right leg. She then takes another drag.

Q. "I hope you come to realize that sooner, rather than later."

She rolls her eyes.

Q. "We can't live our lives based on *'would haves, could haves or should haves'*."

A. "How 'bout *whatevers?* That works for me."

Q. "Maddison was obviously carrying deep secrets and pain long before you two ever met."

Kristyn says nothing. All she can do is choke down the truth with the help of a very bitter tasting Mocha Coffee.

Q. "You only knew the things Maddison wanted you to know about her."

A: "I suppose she could say the same 'bout me. I mean if she were here. *Which*, she's not."

Kristyn then puts out her cigarette.

Q. "It is not your fault what happened to Maddison. Her pain started long ago. You need to understand that."

A feeling of relief washes over Kristyn helping to remove some of the guilt she has been carrying over Maddison's suicide.

'I would be lying if I said right now, I did not want to cut after talking 'bout Maddison. A part of me really, really wants to cut. But I am going to do my best not to for Maddison. And maybe a little for me, too.'

Three hours and several cuts on the right thigh later:

'Dammit I fucked-up, again!'

chapter thirty

Q.   "Have you ever told your parents about being bullied?"

She replies sharply.

A.   "No."

Q. "Why not?"

'Why?'

A. "They wouldn't understand."

Q. "Do you know if Maddison ever told her parents about being bullied?"

'How would I know for sure? Huh? I'm just now realizing, Maddison kept things from me. It makes me mad and sad at the same time. I feel like she didn't trust me or something. But then I also feel bad for feeling mad and sad 'bout it because I kept stuff from her, too. I'm such a hypocritical douche!'

A. "She didn't."

Q. "How do you know?"

A. "Maddison comes...."

'Sorry I'm spilling some of your secrets, Madd.'

A. "I mean, came, from a super-strict house. Showing weakness of any kind..."

She shakes her head side-to-side.

A. "...unacceptable."

Q. "Did Maddison ever express to you how she felt about living in such a strict environment?"

A. "She hated it. She always felt like she could never be what her parents expected her to be."

Q. "What were their expectations of her?"

'How should I know? I'm just guessing. I hope you know that.'

A. "Straight A's. Work. Join every club the school offered. Get accepted early by every top college you apply to."

Q. "How do you think that type of pressure affected Maddison?"

A. "She was miserable. I failed to help her when she needed me."

Q. "How do you feel you failed Maddison?"

A. "I was more focused on trying to sort my own issues. I think we both liked to use distractions to help forget the bad stuff. I know I did."

Q. "Distractions? What do you mean?"

A. "Drinking pints until we vomited. Smoking spliff and then gorging ourselves on sweets. Taking hits of MDMA and dancing our asses off to techno at a club. And boys. Lots of mindless shagging and making out."

Q. "What attracts you to those things?"

Kristyn giggles.

A. "It's fun."

Q. "You find sex, drugs, alcohol and random sex with boys' fun?"

A. "Depends on what I see once their trousers drop past their knees."

She winks.

A. "Actually, I was remembering something."

Q. "Care to share?"

Kristyn giggles a bit more, than regains her composure.

A. "Maddison and I snuck into this party one time and got 'pissed off our faces' on larger."

She sighs.

A. "I remember standing up against the wall, sipping on flat beer from a red solo cup, watching these 'popular' drunk knob heads acting stupid. I began questioning why I longed to be 'round such losers."

Q. "Did you and Maddison leave the party after your realization?"

'I wish. I was so bored. And, that flat beer tasted like panther piss. I'm fairly certain, my liver will exact some form of revenge for that night in the future.'

A. "No, because Maddison was having a jolly time chatting up some guy."

Kristyn's tone drops an octave.

A. "Then…Claire happened."

Q. "The girl who bullied you in the past?"

A. "She started demanding Maddison and I leave the party. I think the guy Maddison had been talking to might have been her boyfriend or something."

Kristyn snickers.

A. "That dozy cow had the nerve to call us whores. Quite an ironic statement coming from Claire."

Q. "How so?"

A. "Claire shags everyone. She's notorious for it. Yet, she's worshipped by *everyone.*"

She huffs in anger.

A. "While girls like Maddison and I are treated like slags for doing the same thing."

Q. "You should feel sorry for Claire."

'Have you lost your fucking mind? Have you not heard one word I've said 'bout that bitch?'

Q. "Claire is lost like you."

She becomes terse.

A.   "Fuck, Claire! She put Maddison and I through hell."

Kristyn crosses her arms.

A.   "Let that cow wander, forever lost in a pasture for all I care."

Q.   "To heal, you must forgive, Kristyn."

Kristyn grunts.

'To diet, you must stop eating chocolate cake. I don't see that happening anytime soon.'

A.   "Anyway, back to that night."

Q.   "Please, continue."
A.   "Claire took a swing at Maddison but missed. Maddison then slapped Claire so hard, she lost her balance and fell with her legs up in the air, putting her white laced knickers on immediate display. Everyone laughed and snapped pictures."

Q.   "How did Claire respond to Maddison's attack?"

A.   "I don't know because Maddison grabbed my hand and we bolted out of there."

Q.   "Did Claire come after you?"

A.   "And risk breaking a heel on her *Jimmy-Choo* shoe? *Um,* no."

Q.   "What happened at school the following Monday, after the party?"

A.   "Pictures of Claire's knickers were all over social media. Oh, and I got a big bruise on my upper arm."

Q.   "From whom?"

A.   "One of Claire's bitch clones punched me in the cafeteria during lunch hour."

Q.   "Who hit you?"

A.   "This girl, Amber. She tries so hard to be like Claire. She acts like a minion awaiting her next assignment from the queen bee herself. Amber is obsessed with Claire. It's kind of creepy and pitiful at the same time."

Q.   "Why did Amber punch you? Did Claire tell her to?"

A.   "Amber said I looked at her funny. I didn't. I was pissed 'bout an algebra test I had just failed. So, when Amber smarted off something to me, I did the same thing back to her. Then, she punched my arm."

Q.   "Were you and Amber suspended for fighting?"

A.   *"Nah,* when security came over, I lied."

Q.   "Why did you lie about being assaulted?"

A.   "Telling on Amber would have only made things worse for me."

If that's even possible.'

Q.   "What did you tell the security guard?"

A.   "I told him we were rehearsing for a school project. Amber
    followed my lead. He believed us and left."

She coughs.

A.   "As soon as the security guard turned his back, Amber threw
    me up against the wall and warned if I ever looked her way
    again, I was going to get it much worse."

*'I should have punched her back. I'm just not as brave as Maddison when
it comes to confrontations. Pussy…party of one.'*

*Kristyn stands up and stretches her arms above her head, revealing scars
across her stomach. She quickly pulls her shirt back down.*
*'I think all that talking earlier 'bout the party and drinking flat beer peaked
my bladder's interest.'*

A.   "Can we take a break now? I need to pee."

Q.   "Of course."

chapter thirty-one

Q. "What sort of things made Maddison happy?"

A. "I thought these sessions were 'bout me."

Q. "They are."

A.   "So, why do you keep bringing up, Maddison, then?"

Q.   "Maddison's influence and suicide have a lot to do with your self-harming behavior."

You forgot to mention Jamey, Claire, Amber, the other Posh Miss Perfects, Ian Rhodes, Seth, other nameless, faceless boys, the planet and everyone on it.'

She groans.

A.   "I was cutting and doing other stuff to myself before she died."

Q.   "But you were also self-harming while she was alive. And she is the one you learned self-harming from."

'I am seriously relating to the pressure a pus-filled zit feels right before it bursts.'

A.   *'Fuckin' hell. She taught me how to do one thing. That's it."*

Q.   "Whenever I seem to speak a truth about your life, you become upset. Why?"

Kristyn crosses her arms and glares.

A.   "What truth? My life is based on lies."

She postures with indignation.

A. "ALL LIES!"

Q. "What sort of lies? Give me an example of a lie you tell yourself."

She ponders.

A. "That cutting will take away my pain."

Q. "Self-harming is not a solution to your problem. Can you not see that?"

She waxes sarcasm.

A. "What if it is a solution to me?"

Kristyn then lifts the right corner of her mouth and sneers.

A. "It's my choice how I see it. Right?"

Q. "Yes. But that does not mean you are correct."

Kristyn shakes her head.

'I should have known there was a catch to the choice thing. I knew it was too good to be true.'

A. "Cutting helps me deal. It's not like I'm hurting anyone."

Q. "Just yourself. Do you ever think about yourself?"

A. *"Whatever. It doesn't matter. I don't matter."*

Q. "Are you saying you do not care about hurting yourself?"

A. "Why should I? No one else does."

Q.   "That is not true. There are people who care about you."

Kristyn makes a repetitive circular motion with her right index finger.

A.   "Yeah. Yeah. Yeah."

Q.   "Let's get back to discussing Maddison."

'Why can't you leave her alone?'

Q.   "How was she acting weeks before she died?"

Kristyn crosses her right leg over her left.

A.   "I remember she became withdrawn from everything, including me."

Q.   "How did her distant behavior make you feel?"

A.   "I don't know. I guess, hurt, alone and a little confused."

Kristyn then lights up a cigarette.

A.   "I never thought she'd take things as far as she did."

'Why did you push me away, M.? Why didn't you tell me what was going on inside of that beautiful fucked up head of yours?'

A.   "Maybe if I had said something, anything…"

She takes a drag.

A.   "*Shit.* I don't know."

Q. "You think if you said something, Maddison would still be here."

Kristyn sheepishly looks up and whispers.

A. *"Maybe."*

Q. "You cannot continue blaming yourself for what Maddison chose to do, Kristyn."

A. *"I choose to."*

Having to face the reality about what happened to Maddison in the upcoming sessions has Kristyn feeling more stressed than usual.

'The weather is complete shit tonight. Endless thunderstorms. One right after the other. No going out dancing tonight. Figures it would happen when I really need to forget 'bout Maddison for a little while. My mind can't handle the truth 'bout what she did. Nor my incredible feelings of guilt.'

Kristyn rummages through her panty drawer and underneath a pair of black laced thong knickers, she finds some leftover MDMA.

'I hate this fucking thong. It's like having a piece of string up my ass 24/7. As if I don't have enough things up my ass as it is.'

She tosses the panties in the rubbish bin. But not just because they are uncomfortable to wear. They were also worn the last time she shagged Jamey — the guy who has her heart wrapped around his finger and her head completely fucked up.

'Tosser!'

Kristyn plugs in her cat ear headphones, drops some MDMA and prepares to forget about her life as the Trance mix, she pulled up on her iPod begins to play the first song, 'Smoke Machine'.

She dances for a few hours, before finally collapsing in the bed. Too tired to dream. Too tired to think. Too tired to care about anything.

'Cheers!'

chapter thirty-two

Q. "What is on your mind today, Kristyn?"

'As if you don't already know. Dozy cow.'

A. "Maddison"

Q. "Let's spend this session working on accepting what happened to Maddison and then how to start letting go of the survivor's guilt you are carrying."

A. "Oh, just like that, *huh?*"

She snaps her fingers.

A. "And I'll be over it."

Q. "That is not what I said."

A. "*Whatever.*"

She opens a bottle of water and chugs half of it down.

Q. "How did you learn about what happened to Maddison?"

Kristyn stares down at the floor for a minute and then looks up.

'Will this torment ever end?'

A. "Maddison had rung me up and wanted to come over. She had gone to Goodwill and found some 1980's skirts made of this tacky shiny silver material. She wanted to turn the skirts into a train for a dress we had been working on for Prom."

Q. "How was Maddison's mood that day?"

A. "She was smiling. I hadn't seen her happy in a long time."

'Dammit, Kristyn. You should have known something was tits up with her right then. Why didn't you see it? Why?'

A.   "A counselor said sometimes when a person decides to end their life, it's not uncommon for them to act happy 'round their mates and family right before they do it."

Q.   "Did the counselor explain to you why that type of behavior happens?"

A.   "She rattled off something 'bout the person feeling relief. Like they see an end to their pain."

She waves her hands.

A.   "Something like that."

Kristyn tugs at her bottom lip, trying to remove a strand of hair stuck to her strawberry flavored lip gloss. She eventually gets it and then wipes her lip gloss-stained fingers on her jeans.

Q.   "What happened after Maddison arrived at your house?"

A.   "We worked on the dress for a bit. There was one more piece of material left to be sewed on, but Maddison had to get home. I didn't think anything of it knowing how strict her Dad was."

She flashes back in her mind, to that last moment with Maddison.

A.   "She hugged me really tight before she left, told me she loved me, gave me a kiss on the cheek and…"

Kristyn takes a deep breath, lets it out and then whispers.

A.   *"She was gone."*

172

Current Mood!

Fuck! Fuck! Fuck! Fuck! Fuck! Fuck! Fuck! Fuck! Fuck! Fuck!
Fuck! Fuck! Fuck! Fuck! Fuck! Fuck! Fuck! Fuck! Fuck! Fuck!
Fuck! Fuck! Fuck! Fuck! Fuck! Fuck! Fuck! Fuck! Fuck! Fuck!
Fuck! Fuck! Fuck! Fuck! Fuck! Fuck! Fuck! Fuck! Fuck! Fuck!
Fuck! Fuck! Fuck! Fuck! Fuck! Fuck! Fuck! Fuck! Fuck! Fuck!
Fuck! Fuck! Fuck! Fuck! Fuck! Fuck! Fuck! Fuck! Fuck! Fuck!
Fuck! Fuck! Fuck! Fuck! Fuck! Fuck! Fuck! Fuck! Fuck! Fuck!
Fuck! Fuck! Fuck! Fuck! Fuck! Fuck! Fuck! Fuck! Fuck! Fuck!
Fuck! Fuck! Fuck! Fuck! Fuck! Fuck! Fuck! Fuck! Fuck! Fuck!
Fuck! Fuck! Fuck! Fuck! Fuck! Fuck! Fuck! Fuck! Fuck! Fuck!
Fuck! Fuck! Fuck! Fuck! Fuck! Fuck! Fuck! Fuck! Fuck! Fuck!
Fuck! Fuck! Fuck! Fuck! Fuck! Fuck! Fuck! Fuck! Fuck! Fuck!
Fuck! Fuck! Fuck! Fuck! Fuck! Fuck! Fuck! Fuck! Fuck! Fuck!
Fuck! Fuck! Fuck! Fuck! Fuck! Fuck! Fuck! Fuck! Fuck! Fuck!
Fuck! Fuck! Fuck! Fuck! Fuck! Fuck! Fuck! Fuck! Fuck! Fuck!
Fuck! Fuck! Fuck! Fuck! Fuck! Fuck! Fuck! Fuck! Fuck! Fuck!
Fuck! Fuck! Fuck! Fuck! Fuck! Fuck! Fuck! Fuck! Fuck! Fuck!
Fuck! Fuck! Fuck! Fuck! Fuck! Fuck! Fuck! Fuck! Fuck! Fuck!
Fuck! Fuck! Fuck! Fuck! Fuck! Fuck! Fuck! Fuck! Fuck! Fuck!
Fuck! Fuck! Fuck! Fuck! Fuck! Fuck! Fuck! Fuck! Fuck! Fuck!
Fuck! Fuck! Fuck! Fuck! Fuck! Fuck! Fuck! Fuck! Fuck! Fuck!
Fuck! Fuck! Fuck! Fuck! Fuck! Fuck! Fuck! Fuck! Fuck! Fuck!

Fuck! Fuck! Fuck! Fuck! Fuck! Fuck! Fuck! Fuck! Fuck! Fuck!
Fuck! Fuck! Fuck! Fuck! Fuck! Fuck! Fuck! Fuck! Fuck! Fuck!
Fuck! Fuck! Fuck! Fuck! Fuck! Fuck! Fuck! Fuck! Fuck! Fuck!
Fuck! Fuck! Fuck! Fuck! Fuck! Fuck! Fuck! Fuck! Fuck! Fuck!
Fuck! Fuck! Fuck! Fuck! Fuck! Fuck! Fuck! Fuck! Fuck! Fuck!
Fuck! Fuck! Fuck! Fuck! Fuck! Fuck! Fuck! Fuck! Fuck! Fuck!
Fuck! Fuck! Fuck! Fuck! Fuck! Fuck! Fuck! Fuck! Fuck! Fuck!
Fuck! Fuck! Fuck! Fuck! Fuck! Fuck! Fuck! Fuck! Fuck! Fuck!
Fuck! Fuck! Fuck! Fuck! Fuck! Fuck! Fuck! Fuck! Fuck! Fuck!
Fuck! Fuck! Fuck! Fuck! Fuck! Fuck! Fuck! Fuck! Fuck! Fuck!
Fuck! Fuck! Fuck! Fuck! Fuck! Fuck! Fuck! Fuck! Fuck! Fuck!
Fuck! Fuck! Fuck! Fuck! Fuck! Fuck! Fuck! Fuck! Fuck! Fuck!
Fuck! Fuck! Fuck! Fuck! Fuck! Fuck! Fuck! Fuck! Fuck! Fuck!
Fuck! Fuck! Fuck! Fuck! Fuck! Fuck! Fuck! Fuck! Fuck! Fuck!
Fuck! Fuck! Fuck! Fuck! Fuck! Fuck! Fuck! Fuck! Fuck! Fuck!
Fuck! Fuck! Fuck! Fuck! Fuck! Fuck! Fuck! Fuck! Fuck! Fuck!
Fuck! Fuck! Fuck! Fuck! Fuck! Fuck! Fuck! Fuck! Fuck! Fuck!
Fuck! Fuck! Fuck! Fuck! Fuck! Fuck! Fuck! Fuck! Fuck! Fuck!

Fuck everything!

Fuck everyone!

Fuck life!

Go fuck yourself, Kristyn!

chapter thirty-three

Kristyn enters the room wearing her typical scowl.

'I already told three people to fuck off today. If you're smart, you'll watch what you say to me or be number four.'

Q. "You seem angry."

She holds up four fingers.

'Fuck off!'

A. "I am."

She slams her purse down and digs around inside it for a tissue to blow her nose.

Q. "Who are you angry at?"

A. "Maddison."

Q. "Is it because we talked about her last session?"

'Seriously?'

A. "Ya think?"

Q. "Why are you angry at Maddison?"

A. "I miss her, but I also want to beat the crap out of her. Why did she give up? How could she do something like that to me? To her family? To herself?"

A tear slips out of Kristyn's right eye, navigates down her sturdy cheekbone and onto her lap, where it blends into her jeans.

Q. "I'm afraid only Maddison holds the key to the real answer because unfortunately she did not leave a note, right?"

Kristyn releases a loud sigh.

A. *"Right."*

She then blows her nose.

Q. "What happened the day you learned Maddison died?"

Kristyn's breathing begins to speed up. She is feeling anxious having to relive that horrible day. She pulls on a few strands of hair as she talks.

'God help me! Please! I mean if you're not too busy giving some douche in Hollywood another mansion or something.'

A. "It was the morning after I last saw Maddison. I was walking down the hall at school between second and third period, heading to my locker. I noticed everyone was staring at me and whispering. By the time I reached my locker, I knew Maddison was gone."

Q. "How did you know?"

A. "My school counselor and another lady were waiting for me at my locker. They both looked sad. I mean, really sad."

Kristyn takes a sip of water.

Q. "Did your counselor speak to you then?"

'Why do I have to remember this? I don't want to. I don't like reliving this. I really wish I could get drunk right on lager, even though I hate it.'

A. "No one said a word. All I remember is screaming out *"No"* a bunch of times before my knees gave out and I fell to the floor sobbing uncontrollably."

She fights back more tears.

A. "I couldn't breathe."

Kristyn then begins to lightly hyperventilate.

Q. "Slow down your breathing, Kristyn. Exhale. Breathe in through your nose to the count of four. Hold your breath to the count of seven."

She does as she is told.

Q. "Now exhale out of your nose to the count of eight."

She exhales and her body begins to relax. Her breathing soon returns to normal.

Q. "Better?"

She whispers.

A.   *"I think so."*

Q.   "Are you ready to continue?"

'Not really…but whatever.'

A.   "I remember my counselor and the other lady, who I found out was a grief counselor, pulling me up off the floor and taking me to the office."

Q.   "Did they fetch the nurse?"

A.   "No. One of them did ask if I wanted my parents."

Q.   "Did you?"

A.   "No."

Q.   "Why did you not want your parents with you during such a traumatic time?"

'Down inside I suppose I wanted my mum with me. But I just couldn't bring myself to reach out to anyone. The walls were closing in around me. I didn't know what to do. I wanted to run, but I didn't know where to go.'

A.   "I was afraid my parents would find out 'bout what I'd been up to."

Q.   "You mean, your self-harming?"

A.   "I'm a total selfish bitch for thinking like that, *huh?*"

Q. "Not really."

'I feel like a jerk'

Q. "What happened next?"

'I wish I could just take you back in time to that day like the 'Ghost of Christmas Past', so you could see it for yourself instead of making me talk 'bout it. Again. And again. And again.'

She pulls lightly on her hair to avoid unleashing a tirade of profanity laced objections to the line of questioning.

A. "I was really freaking out 'bout all of it."

Q. "That is understandable."

A. "No, you don't understand."

Q. "What don't I understand?"

A. "I was worried more 'bout me, than 'bout what happened to Maddison. I feared being found out."

'Wow! I really am a selfish piece of shit.'

Q. "You were in shock."

A. *"Whatever.* I finally demanded they tell me 'bout what happened to Maddison or I wouldn't answer any more of their questions."

Q. "Did they tell you how she died?"

Kristyn breaks eye contact and whispers her reply.

A.   *"Yeah. Her mum found her."*

Kristyn then begins to cry uncontrollably. The session ends for the day.

chapter thirty-four

Q. "Have you spoken to Maddison's family since her death?"

A. "No. I can't. I'm not ready, yet."

Q. "Why not?"

A. "I'm afraid of the questions her mum might ask."

Q. "Have you spoken to your school counselor lately about Maddison?"

Kristyn quickly shakes her head side to side and waves her right-hand side to side, too.

A. "Not since the day I told them both to fuck off before I left school."

Q. "Why did you leave school?"

A. "I wanted to be alone. I needed to deal with what happened in my own way."

Q. "In other words, you needed to self-harm."

A. *"Cheers."*

Kristyn rubs her left hand across her stomach.

Q. "Does your stomach hurt?"

A. "No."

Q. "Is that where you self-harmed the day you learned Maddison died?"

Kristyn looks down at her stomach before softly replying.

A. *"Yeah."*

'You don't understand the pain I was in at the time. Stop looking at me like the weak, pathetic loser I feel I am. I get enough judgmental looks at school.'

Q. "Where did you go after you left school that day?"

A. "Home."

Q. "Why home?"

A.   "My parents are never there."

Q. "Why are your parents never home?"

She looks around the room.

A.   "They both work a lot. I think my mum has two jobs right now. I'm not sure."

Q.   "Are you upset by their absence?"

A.   "Sometimes. But I get it."

'You gotta do what you gotta do sometimes. Like it or not. For instance, the time I had to shag Ian for some spliff. He was the only one holding. I didn't have any money. I didn't want to do it, but I needed to get stoned to forget. Nothing else was helping me. I tried cutting. I tried purging after eating almost an entire cake by myself. Oh, what a bad day it was. My birthday. Maddison and I always did something special together on our birthdays. It was my first birthday without her. So...'

A.   "It wouldn't have mattered if my parents were home that day or not."

Q.   "Why not? It is quite common for children to seek the comfort of a parent when they are sick or hurting."

She spitefully sneers.

A.   "I didn't want to be comforted by my mummy or daddy."

Q.   "What did you want?"

A.   "To be alone. I had these fucked-up emotions swirling 'round inside my head. I never felt pain like that before in my life. I just wanted it gone."

She huffs.

A.   "Grief's the worst feeling in the world. It's like you're suddenly emptied out and all that's left is a big hole that can't be filled no matter how many tears you cry, how much you cut, how much you purge or how many boys you shag. Nothing helps. I hope I never feel pain like that again. Ever!"

Q. "Unfortunately, pain is a part of life."

She runs her tongue across her teeth.

'Well, all I have to say to pain and those who cause it – 'Go fuck yourselves!"

A. *"Great, more good news."*

Q. "You should not have been alone that day, Kristyn."

'I know. I screwed-up, again. Did it wrong. Cocked it up. Made a mess. Nothing new to see here. Keep moving along.'

A. "I knew if I saw my parents, Maddison's death would be real. I mean, *really… real.* And I just couldn't…"

She turns her attention to the window but is so lost in thoughts about Maddison, she fails to notice a red cardinal perched upon the windowsill.

Q. "Did you self-harm once you arrived at home?"

A. "No, but my overwhelmed emotions made me puke."

Q. "I am sorry you got sick."

A. "After I came out of the bathroom, I saw it."

The horrible feelings she felt that day begin encroaching on her memory like the 'Blob' did in the 1958 movie, when it surrounded the diner. No chance of escaping the inevitable.

Q. "What did you see when you came out of the bathroom?"

A. "The dress Maddison and I had worked on the day before. It was hanging on the closet door where she had left it."

Q. "How did you feel when you saw it?"

A. "Angry. I was angry at Maddison for leaving me. And I was angry at myself, too."

Q. "Why did you feel anger towards yourself?"

A. "I felt like I had failed my best friend."

'Because you did fail her. Loser!'

Q. "You did not fail Maddison, Kristyn."

'Oh, yes, I fucking did.'

A. "I remember grabbing the dress and cussing out Maddison with each tear I made into the fabric."

She sniffles.

A. "I couldn't understand why she did it. Why didn't she talk to me?"

Kristyn blows her nose.

A. "Then, I realized I was destroying the last memory I had of her."

Kristyn dabs at her eyes with a tissue.

Q. "Did you want to self-harm?"

Kristyn blows her nose.

A. "Of course. I was suffocating. I had so much stuff to let out. But I had to wait."

Q. "Why did you have to wait? You were alone in the house, right?"

A. "I was sure the school had called my parents. I knew they would be coming home soon."

Q. "What happened when your parents did come home?"

Her defenses begin to crumble as she finally begins to open-up for the first time about losing, Maddison.

A. "I was scared. I wasn't sure what they were going to do."

Q. "What do you mean?"

A. "They had this look in their eyes. I think they were afraid I was going to kill myself, too. I was so afraid my cutting secret would be found out if they chose to admit me to the hospital out of panic."

Q. "How did you handle the situation?"

A. "I told my parents what they wanted to hear."

Q. "What did you say?"

A.   "That I was okay. I just wanted to be alone and listen to music and try to process everything."

Kristyn stretches her lanky body, reaching her arms upward as if trying to touch the ceiling. She notices a water stain in the far corner from a prior roof leak.

A.   "My emotions were so jumbled. I needed to feel anything other than what I was feeling at the time, you know?"

Q.   "What were you feeling?"

A.   "Anger, then nothing, then anger, again."

Q.   "Anger towards Maddison was understandable."

A.   "I wasn't angry at Maddison. I mean, I was. But I was really angry at God."

Q.   "Why were you angry at God?"

A.   "I blamed Him for taking Maddison away."

Q.   "God did not take Maddison away, Kristyn. Maddison took herself away."

A.   "Well, He didn't exactly give her a reason to stay, now did He?"

Q.   "What do you mean?"

A.   "It's like God didn't have her back. He abandoned her."

Q.   "Did you have personal knowledge of what her relationship with God was?"

Kristyn glances out the window.

A.   "No."

Q.   "Then how do you know God did not try to be there for her?"

A.   "Claire and her skank friends put Maddison through hell. I've yet to see God punish them for what they did to her."

Q.   "Claire and her friends will eventually reap what they sowed."

Kristyn rolls her eyes and crosses her arms.

A.   "Yeah, right."

Q.   "God will right the wrong. Trust Him to do it."

A.   "Oh, so what? I'm supposed to sit here and wait for the *Almighty* to do His thing whenever He feels like it?"

Q.   "It is in His timing, not yours. You need to forgive them for what they did to you and to Maddison so you can move on in a healthy direction."

Kristyn lets out a laugh and nearly chokes on phlegm that runs from her nose down the back of her throat due to the crying. She coughs a few times.

A.   "Are you serious? Forgive those bitches after what *they've* done? To Maddison? To me?"

Q. "Yes."

A. "Should I also bake them brownies, too, while I'm at it?"

Q. "You are acting ridiculous."

A. "So are you. Forgive – *pah*! I'd rather tell them all to piss off!"

Q. "Hate is a terrible burden to carry, Kristyn. It can make you sick. You need to release the anger and forgive those who have hurt you. It is how you heal. When you do not let anger go, you only hurt yourself. It is like making a drink laced with poison, intended for your enemy, yet you are the one who ingests it. Forgive, heal and move on."

A. "But look at what they did to Maddison. To me."

Q. "Maddison chose to kill herself. You chose to get help. They chose to be cruel. Life is about choices."

A. "But Maddison never would have had that choice to make if she hadn't been bullied by those bitches."

Q. "You cannot know that for sure. Maddison kept secrets from you. You kept secrets from her. You need to consider that maybe Maddison's issues went beyond just being bullied. Remember the scars you first saw on her stomach? She was obviously dealing with issues and self-harming long before you came into her life."

She mumbles.

A. *"Whatever."*

Q. "You are still here for a reason, Kristyn."

Kristyn snaps back with sarcasm.

A.   "Don't you mean, by *choice?*"

chapter thirty-five

Q. "Are you ready to move forward with your life, Kristyn?"

A. "And deal with more disappointments? No thanks."

Q. "We talked about forgiveness the other day."

A. "So, what."

Q. "If you would like to move forward with your life, you are going to have to find a way to forgive those who have done you and Maddison wrong. You also need to find a way to forgive Maddison. And you need to find a way to forgive yourself. Forgiveness is the first step towards healing."

A. "So, I've heard."

Q. "I think it bears repeating."

A. "What the fuck do I have to forgive myself for? What'd I do?"

I mean, besides suck up oxygen that could have been used by someone worthy. Sorry 'bout that, cruel world.'

Q. "You clearly have a lot of anger still locked up inside of you."

A. "You would, too."

Q. "Forgiveness is…"

A. "Bollocks."

Q. "It is a way to…"

A. "Well, I can't see myself walking up to Claire saying, *'I forgive you'* and really mean it. I can, however, see myself wrecking her nose job with my fist."

She then punches her left hand with her right fist.

Q. "You forgive with your heart. No words ever need be spoken to the person you are forgiving. If you feel the need, you can also write them a letter, expressing your feelings and then tear it up."

'Well, I don't have a heart anymore. Thank you, Jamey. Thank you, Maddison. Oh, and fuck both of you! Selfish pricks! Because of you both, my heart's been shattered beyond repair. So, how exactly is this little plan of forgiveness going to work?'

Q. "Forgiving Claire, Jamey, Maddison and anyone else who hurt you is for your benefit, Kristyn, not theirs."

A. "Not. Gonna. Happen."

Later that night...

Kristyn snuck out of the house and into a club. Well, not really snuck. She knows the bouncer. He ignores the fact she is not legal to get in because she slips him spliff now and then.

Five minutes inside and she spied the hottie she scored some top MDMA from and shagged a while back. The same guy whose name she still can't recall. The same guy she had to shove out of her bedroom window before her mum caught them together.

The music was booming loud. Her heart immediately began beating in time with the bass. The hottie did not disappoint. After dropping some MDMA, Kristyn danced non-stop for hours.

'I felt so free on the dance floor. Like a bird. I was able to spread my wings and let go. Really let go of the pain, Jamey, Maddison. All of it. I never wanted it to stop.'

When the club lights came on, what she had been running from returned. The MDMA was wearing off. She desperately needed another kind of fix.

After leaving the club, she snuck back home and cut in the bathroom. But it felt pointless this time. She did not get the slightest feeling of euphoria or relief. In fact, she felt nothing. It was as if the monster inside was smashed on valium.

'What the fuck is happening to me? Why won't the monster leave, like before?'

She stares down at her thigh and watches a small trail of blood run down it. Still nothing. She chucks the razor blade up into the sink.

'Fuck! I look like I'm ragging."

Suddenly, a light tap is heard on her bedroom windowpane. She cracks the bathroom door and sees it's the MDMA hottie with the shaggy blonde hair. He had climbed up the trellis and onto the roof. She quickly cleans herself up and opens the window so he can climb in.
'May as well have a shag. Nothing else is helping.'

By morning, the MDMA hottie is gone. The shagging was fantastic. However, having to face herself in the mirror becomes an unpleasant task.

'You are a proper whore, indeed. And you still don't remember his name? Brilliant as usual, Kristyn! At least you are consistent with screwing up and making yourself feel worse than the day before. I'll give you that. But only, that.'

chapter thirty-six

Q. "Did you attend Maddison's funeral?"

A. "No."

Q. "Why not?"

A. "Because if I went, she was really gone. I wasn't ready to accept it at the time."

Q. "And now?"

A. "Every day 's still a struggle for me."

She takes a sip of water.

A. "But I visit her grave now and leave purple daffodils."

Q. "Were purple daffodils Maddison's favorite flower?"

She whispers.

A. *"Yeah."*

A.   "Sometimes I'll bring swatches of material I know she would have enjoyed making an outfit from."

Q.   "Do you still sew?"

Why do I feel so guilty 'bout wanting to keep doing fashion without you, Maddison? You're the one who quit on me. I failed you, but I never quit on you. Never.'

A.   "A little."

Q.   "I think that is good."

Kristyn shrugs her shoulders and looks around the room.

A.   *"Maybe."*

Q.   "Designing clothes gives you something positive to focus on."

'Maddison was the real designer. She's the one who had the talent. I only know how to thread a needle. Yeah, because that takes talent. Not!'

A.   *"Whatever.* It's not like anything's changed since she died."

Q.   "You have changed."

'Only my knickers. Not my mind. Not my feelings. And definitely not my attitude.'

A.   *"Yeah.* I'm more depressed than before. If that's even possible."

Q.   "It's understandable. Traumatic events change a person."

A. "You know, the first month after Maddison died, *everyone* sucked up to me. You should have seen it. *They* acted like *they* had lost *their* best friend."

She becomes snarky.

A. "What a bloody joke."

Q. "You have doubts about *their* sincerity?"

A. "*They* never gave a bleeding crap 'bout Maddison. Ever."

Q. "I am sure some must have felt sorry for what happened."

A. "Don't you mean what *they* caused to happen?"

Q. "*They* did not make Maddison kill herself. Maddison killed herself because of issues she had been dealing with long before she ever knew you or *them*."

'You might be right. But I'm not going to lie. It feels good blaming Claire and her douche friends. I still blame myself for not being a better friend and failing to realize you were in so much pain, Maddison.'

A. *"Whatever."*

Q. "Sometimes it takes a shocking event to make a person realize they need to change their bad behavior."

Kristyn plants both feet firmly on the floor and leans forward to emphasize her point.

A. "Maddison was not a sacrificial lamb sent here for wankers to perform a self-righteous ritual to learn right from wrong.

She was a person. My best friend. She didn't deserve to be treated like shit."

Q. "What I said was maybe some of those people who were cruel to her actually feel bad now for how *they* treated her."

Kristyn crosses her arms.

A. "Too little, too late."

Q. "What about forgiveness, Kristyn? Remember?"

Kristyn scoffs.

A. "How can I forget 'bout it when you keep reminding me every two seconds."

chapter thirty-seven

Q.   "Have things settled down at school since Maddison passed away?"

'I wish my emotions would piss off. I'm so tired of feeling this way.'

A.   "It's like Maddison never existed."

Q.   "She still exists. She is in there."

Kristyn glances down at her chest.

A.   "In my boobs?"

Q.   "No, your heart."

She blushes.

A.   "Oh."

'Idiot. Party of one.'

Q.   "It is okay to move on with your life. You have nothing to feel guilty about."

Kristyn mutters under her breath.

A.   *"For some, maybe it is. But not for me."*

Q.   "It does not mean Maddison is not still a part of your life. She is, but in a new way now."

A.   "What do you mean by that?"

Q.   "A memory."

'Stick your memory idea right up your...'

A.   "Well, I don't want a sodding memory. I want Maddison. Here. With. Me. Now."

She takes a deep breath.

A.   "I don't want only the memories we shared. I want to make new ones with her. This isn't fair."

Q.   "I know it's not, Kristyn."

A.   *"Yeah, right."*

Q.   "How are you being treated at school since her passing?"

A.   "You mean her suicide?"

Q.   "You feel comfortable enough to use that word?"

A.   "Not really. But, it's what she did. No point in making what she did sound dainty because it's not."

She drinks some water.

Q.   "Back to my question."

A.   "I'm being treated the same at school. Like crap."

Kristyn glances over at a black and gold Bible sitting on the edge of the table. The cover is hidden beneath a light coating of dust.

A.   "Do you believe?"

Q.   "Do I believe in what?"

Kristyn motions her head at the Bible.

A.   "The Bible?"

Q.   "I'd like to think I do."

A.   "That's funny."

Q.   "What is funny?"

A.   "Based on the dust I see; you haven't opened that Bible in a *long* time."

Q.   "Do you believe in the Bible, Kristyn?"

Kristyn shrugs her shoulders and then looks around the room. She suddenly takes notice of the silence. The cricket she once heard chirping from inside the floor vent has grown quiet.

I wonder if he was able to escape this four-walled prison and he's off somewhere hopping his cares away. Or maybe he died of boredom from listening to tales 'bout my lame ass life.'

A.   "Sometimes."

Q.   "Why only sometimes? What shakes your faith?"

A.   "Depends on what day you ask me."

Q.   "So, you are saying your faith operates like a thermometer, going up and down depending on what is happening in your life at the moment?"

A.   "Isn't that what most people do?"

Q.   "Did you know Jesus was bullied, too?"

She waxes sarcasm.

A.   "Well, if the God's son was bullied, I suppose there's no hope for the rest of us minions stuck here on earth, now is there?"

Q.   "Does it help knowing God's son was picked on, too?"

Kristyn shrugs her shoulders, unsure of how to answer the question.

Q.   "What are your feelings about God?"

A.   "Anger."

Q.   "Why anger?"

A.   "What happened with Maddison. The life He gave me. You know, I never asked to be born or created, or whatever."

Q.   "You do not think you might bear some responsibility in the unhappiness you feel about your life?"

A warmth, brought about by her subconscious, is starting to feel like a pit of hell fire being stoked beneath her butt. She fidgets in her chair.

A.   "I fancy myself more like Saint Augustine."

Q.   "Saint Augustine is an interesting comparison. How so?"

A.   "Kind of good and bad rolled into one. You know."

Q.   "Saint Augustine is a very dangerous combination. Keeping the scales in life balanced towards good in one's life can be rather challenging in the world today."

A.   "I think it makes life not so predictable, despite my scales always tipping more on the bad side than the good."

chapter thirty-eight

Kristyn pinches her left side, and a look of disgust comes on her face. She is rail thin but fails to see herself that way.

A.   "*Ugh!* Shouldn't have eaten that plate of chips. Just look at this disgusting muffin top."

Kristyn raises up her shirt enough to reveal a flat stomach covered with scars put there over losing Maddison. She suddenly realizes her scars are exposed and quickly pulls her turquoise burnout T shirt back down.

Q.   "You think you are fat?"

A.   "Show me a teenage girl who doesn't?"

Q.   "Do you ever use food as a form of punishment?"

'Crap!'

She plays coy.

A.   "What do you mean?"

Q.   "Do you starve yourself? Binge and purge? Or just binge?"

Kristyn shrugs her shoulders.

'Oh, who are you kidding, Kristyn? You've done all three. Hell, you still do one of them. Denial is pointless. May as well come clean.'

A.   "Sometimes."

Q.   "Which of the three do you do?"

'Let's talk 'bout what you do with food, instead.'

A.   "I've done them all. But I only bird-diet now."

Q.   "What do you mean by you bird-diet?"

'I eat frickin' seeds. Geez. What do you think I mean?'

A.   "I go a day or two eating only a handful of food, like crackers or whatever's 'round the house."

Q.   "That is not healthy eating."

She whispers.

A.   *"I know."*

Q.   "You need at least 2,000 calories a day."

A.   "It's supposed to be punishment."

Q.   "How do you see starving yourself as punishment?"

'I don't. Well, wait. That's not entirely true. I do get some feeling of satisfaction knowing I am hurting myself and possibly getting closer to leaving this shitty spinning marble called, earth.'

A. "Just do."

Q. "In my opinion...'

She murmurs.

A. *"Great."*

Q. "Starving yourself of food sounds more like a means of control than a form of punishment."

A. "Figured that one out all on our own, did you?"

Kristyn pulls in her bottom lip and scrapes her bottom teeth across it before jutting it back out.

'You might be right, but I still see depriving myself of food as punishment more than control.'

Q. "Do you get a release, like when you cut, by denying your body food?"

A. "I wish."

'But you should know, I do enjoy making myself squirm, especially when those strong hunger pangs kick in and I'm the one who gets to decide if or when my body gets fed. Yes, I do believe I take some sort of twisted pleasure in it.'

She ponders.
'Wow! Maybe you're right. Maybe it is 'bout control. But I'm not 'bout to let on you're right.'

Q. "It almost sounds like you are bullying yourself."

A. "Maybe I am."

'Maybe I think I deserve it. Maybe I do a better job at bullying myself than they ever could.'

Q. "You mentioned you binge and purge, too."

A. "I used to. But not anymore."

Kristyn grabs three small pieces of hair in the front and begins braiding them.

Q. "How often did you use to binge and purge?"

A. "A few times a week. But, like I said, I stopped."

Q. "What made you stop?"

A. "I didn't want my teeth to fall out from acid erosion. I read 'bout it happening to some girls."

She shudders.

A.   *"Gross."*

Q. "Did you ever binge and purge because of body issues? I only ask because you commented earlier about having a muffin top."

A. "A few times. But I did it mostly for punishment."

Q. "May I ask what you punish yourself for?"

She pauses.

A.   "Existing. What else."

chapter thirty-nine

Q. "I am aware you have been abused physically and emotionally. What about sexual abuse?"

Kristyn pulls at her eyelashes on the right eye and manages to trap one between her finger and thumb. She stares at it.

A. "They say if you find an eyelash in your hand, you're supposed to close your eyes, make a wish, then blow and your wish comes true."

Kristyn closes her eyes.

'I wish Maddison were here right now.'

Q. "Why are you avoiding answering my question?"

A. "Because it's pointless"

Q. "Why?"

A. "Because I haven't been messed with. At least not in the way you think. I have, however, been treated like a sperm jar at a fertility clinic by blokes."

Q. "Why do you allow yourself to be treated in such a disrespectful way?"

'I like boys. Boys like me. So, that's what you do. You have sex. Lots of sex.'

A. "I get confused."

Q. "How do you mean?"

A. "It's like I feel good in the moment with whomever I've hooked up with. But then I feel disgusted afterwards. It's like a thousand showers and a million douches can't wash the *'ick'* feeling away. I don't know why my feelings change. They just do."

'You're such a liar, Kristyn. You know damn well why you feel the way you do after sex. It is because of that tosser ex of yours, Jamey. I mean, he wasn't exactly a fantastic shag. He rather sucked. But your love for him helped you overlook the lack of satisfaction his wee willy ever attempted to give to you. All two minutes of it. Stop being a petty bitch. It was more like five minutes. Whatever! The point is, none of the guys you shag now are him. Even though they do it better. Shh. You still love Jamey. That's the problem. Get honest with yourself. Please. You're driving me batty. Oh, and heart — piss off!'

A parade of past sexual encounters begins creeping out from the shadows of her subconscious and straight into her conscience.

'Ugh!'

Q. "If sex leaves you feeling unfulfilled…"

A. *"Disgusted."*
'How could three minutes fulfill any girl? Asking for a friend.'

Q. "If sex leaves you feeling disgusted afterwards, why
     continue doing it?"

*'How does it go? Oh, yeah. The definition of insanity is doing the same
thing over and again, expecting a different result. So, I'm apparently
insane. Just add it to the list of other fuckups and such; lame, stupid,
whore, etc.'*

A. "Loneliness. Boredom. Self-loathing."

Q. "Have you considered not engaging in sex until you
     understand why it makes you feel so bad afterwards?"

A. "Nope."

Q. "Why not?"

*'Okay. So, do I lie or finally share some truth 'bout myself? I know if I
don't start sharing, I'll never get out of this room. I'm barely existing in as
it is. But I'm afraid. What if the person I really am is someone I can't stand
and never will? Then what do I do?'*

A. "I'm just a girl who wants to be loved and feel acceptable."

Q. "Yet, sex appears to offer you the exact opposite."

*'Who cares what it offers. I think it's better if I just shag n' go. No risk of
becoming emotionally attached that way.'*

A. "Like what?"

Q. "Self-hatred. Self-rejection."
*She gets up from the chair and walks over to the window. There is nothing
to see but her own pitiful reflection staring back at her in the windowpane.*

The squirrels are tucked away inside their nests. No running around the tree trunk on this dreary, rain-fueled day.

Q. "Sex and love are very different from one another."

She walks back to the dreaded red chair and sits down.

A. "If I close my eyes right now, I can see different boys on top of me. I can remember their smell and their sounds. Their breaths coming faster, harder. I can hear the many lies they spoke over, and over again only to get into my knickers. And yet, knowing what I know, I still choose to block it out whenever a cute boy flirts me up. I hate it."

Q. "So, why do you think you continue doing it?"

Kristyn shrugs her shoulders and takes a drink.

Q. "A shoulder shrug is not an answer."

A. "It's the only answer I can give you."

Q. "You cannot expect someone to respect, let alone love you, while engaging in sexual behavior in the school parking lot between classes, sexting or sleeping with someone right away. Those types of relationships are certain to end before even beginning because there is no foundation to build something from. There is no respect. By continuing to engage in this type of behavior, you are setting yourself up to be hurt and used. You are only damaging yourself."

A. "I told you. I don't sext."

Q. "My apologies."

Kristyn drops her head into her hands and shakes her head side to side.

A. "Why am I like this?"

Q. "You are in the process of finding out."

A. "I'm not sure I want to know, now."

chapter forty

Q. "I would like to resume talking about your self-harming."

She whines.

A. "*Ugh!* Can't we talk 'bout something else?"

Q. "Self-harming is the main reason you are here."

A. "But we've talked 'bout other stuff before."

Q. "Have you noticed how it all ties together?"

She mutters.

A. "*Whatever.*"

Q. "Does participating in self-harm help give you some control over your life, Kristyn?"

A. "Well, I get to decide how and where I cut. But not when. I have no choice over that part, and it sucks."

Q. "What do you mean you have no choice?"

A. "If I'm suddenly stressed over something, I have to do something right then or explode from the overwhelming bad feelings that overtake me. You know, the monster."

Q. "So, for you, self-harming is the answer to fixing the pain you feel?"

A. "No. Cutting just is."

Q. "What sort of items have you used to harm yourself with?"

Kristyn digs into her purse and retrieves a razor blade from a small mint tin. She holds it up and half-smiles.

A. "Obviously my first choice."

Q. "Put that away, please."

Kristen places the razor into the box and drops it back into her purse.

'I wasn't going to use it. Geez. If you paid attention to anything I've said in these sessions, you'd know I don't like an audience when I cut.'

Q. "What else have you used?"

Kristyn stares up at the ceiling for a moment. She then begins listing off items, raising a finger into the air with each spoken object.

She begins by raisings her index finger.

A. "Broken glass."
She raises her middle finger next.

A. "A knife."
She raises her ring finger.

A.   "The edge of the hard-plastic package my headphones came in."

Her pinky finger is raised last.

A.   "Stolen blades from the art class."

She lowers her fingers and hand.

A.   "Pretty much anything that slices skin. I've even used my fingernails. They don't do much damage though, unless I sharpen them into knife-like points. But even then, it's hard to make myself bleed enough to feel a true release."

Q.   "Why use self-harm to cope with your pain? There are healthier options available."

A.   "Because I deserve to feel the pain."

Q.   "You do not deserve to feel pain."

A.   "I don't have to breathe either but...."

Kristyn takes in a deep breath and exhales.

A.   "*Oops...*looks like I just did."

Am I Drowning?
Sure, feels like it to me.

A fish out of water

or one floating at the top

Both gasping for breath, manslaughter

wishing the pain inside of me would stop.

chapter forty-one

Kristyn retrieves a stick of gum from her purse, shoves it into her mouth and begins chewing on the sugary goodness at a feverish pace.

Q. "How do you see self-harming as a way to heal from emotional pain?"

A. "Because when my flesh spreads apart, my twisted emotions spill out. They're now free."

Kristyn blows a bubble and then pops it with her teeth.

Q. "But what you just described is only a temporary feeling, right?"

A. *"Yeah."*

She hesitates.

A. "The fucked-up feelings, the monster inside, always returns."

Q. "Tell me about the monster."

A. "What do you want to know?"

Q. "What does the monster mean to you?"

A. "It's just my continuous fucked-up emotions that are always with me. Nothing more."

Kristyn runs her hand through her hair.

Q. "What about the physical pain you cause to yourself while releasing your emotional pain or the monster as you like to call it?"

A. "It's just part of the journey."

Q. "How does the journey make you feel?"

A. "Shame."

Q. "Why shame?"

Kristyn holds up her wrists.

A. "I can't deal with my emotions…*obviously.*"

Kristyn pops another bubble with her gum.

A. "I'm reminded of how weak and pathetic I truly am. It pisses me off."

Q. "Why not just stop doing it?"

A. "Because the bad feelings are always there. They never go away. I never get the control no matter how much I cut."

Q. "And you would like to have control of the monster?"

She lifts her shirt, showing her stomach, before showing her wrists again.

A. "Wouldn't you?"

chapter forty-two

Q. "How are your grades in school?"

'I'd rather drive rusty nails up my fingernails than go to school. Wish mum and dad could homeschool me instead.'

A. "Not good."

Q. "Are you failing?"

'At life? Definitely. School? I'm barely passing right now.'

A. "It's hard to focus since Maddison..."

Q. "That is understandable. This last year has been very difficult for you in many ways."

Jamey. Maddison. Jamey. Maddison. Jamey Maddison. Jamey. Bugger!'

A. "I'm trying my best to pass because I want to graduate and leave New York."

Q. "Is there a University you would like to attend?"

More like, is there a University desperate enough to accept my shitty grades and matching loser disposition?'

Q.   "Do you want to go to a University, Kristyn?"

Kristyn half-smiles.

A.   "Maddison and I were planning to major in fashion together. It's weird making plans without her now."

Q.   "Life goes on whether we want it to or not."

Kristyn drops her eyes and her voice.

A.   *"I want life to go back before Maddison died."*

She can feel the tears starting to build-up. She is angry over this moment of weakness and quickly reprimands herself.

Don't you cry now, bitch.'

chapter forty-three

A. "My Mum almost found out 'bout my cutting."

Q. "How did that happen?"

A. "She noticed a fresh cut on my upper arm when I was trying on a shirt at *Rack It*. She asked me what happened."

Q. "Did you tell her the truth?"

Kristyn chuckles.

Q. "I will assume not."

'You're such a genius. Did you graduate top of your class or something?'

A. "Of course, I lied."

Q. "Why not tell her the truth?"

A. "I was afraid."

Q. "What lie did you tell her?"

A. "I blamed it on Maddison's cat, Shayne."

Q. "I see."

A. "I'm not sure which felt worse though."

Q. "What?"

A. "The lie I told her or the fact that she believed me."

Q. "Wait. I am confused. How did your cat lie work? According to one of our past sessions, you said you have not spoken to Maddison's parents since her passing. So, how would you have seen Maddison's cat?"

A. "Maddison's mum 's allergic to cats. Shayne used to live in Maddison's room. After she died, her militant brother gave Shayne to me."

Q. "How do you feel having Shayne?"

A. "It helps me feel close to Maddison."

Kristyn giggles.

A. "I talk to Shayne sometimes. She doesn't say much back other than *'meow'*, but I think we understand one another."

Q. "What do you talk to Shayne about?"

A. "Mostly 'bout Maddison. But sometimes I chat her up 'bout catching a spider that's been hiding in my room for a month now. Hate those bloody eight-legged bugs."

Q. "I am sure having Shayne helps fill some of the loneliness you have been feeling since Maddison passed away."

A. "It does, but I still miss her so much."

Q. "It is going to take time to heal."

'Blah! Blah! Blah! Time! I'm so sick of that word, time. It's like serving a prison sentence with no chance for parole.'

Q. "Getting back to your mom almost finding out about your self-harming behavior. How did you feel about your secret behavior almost being exposed?"

'How in the hell do you think I felt? Seriously. And by my mum of all people.'

A. "Freaked out. I mean, some people drink. Some people do drugs. Some people smoke cigarettes. Some people vape. Some people graze on junk food. I do a combo of self-destructive things and then choose to lie 'bout it. I'm not proud of what I do. It's just the way it is."

Q. "How do you plan to fix this problem you have?"

'I don't.'

A. "I was kind of hoping you could tell me."

chapter forty-four

A.   "You think I'm batty because of my scars, don't you?"

Q.   "Do you see yourself as batty?"

'Deflecting my question. Nice.'

A.   "I've read online it's not normal. Those that don't cut see those of us that do cut as batty. Non-cutters treat us like we're barmy or seeking pity."

'Pity can suck it!'

A.   "Nobody understands a cutter except another cutter."

She sighs.

A.   "My scars are my private journal, only without words. I can look at each scar and go right back to that very moment when it was done and remember everything."

'Let's see if this next part shocks you.'

A.   "I've reopened areas where I cut in the past."

Q.   "What provokes you to reopen an old wound?"

'Wow! You don't seem shocked. I'm actually…well, shocked by your lack of shock at what I just admitted to doing.'

A.   "To edit."

Q.   "I do not follow."

Kristyn snarls and stomps both feet onto the floor.

'Fucks sake! It's like I have to spell everything out 'bout myself so you get it. Dozy cow.'

A.   "To release existing pain still trapped inside. Stop being so daft. It's annoying."

Q.   "I have a few more questions about Maddison."

Kristyn rolls her eyes.

'The bullies won't let her rest in peace. Neither will you. Unbelievable.'

A.   "What do you want to know 'bout her now?"

Kristyn lights up a cigarette and tosses the lighter onto the table.

Q.   "You stated you and Maddison never participated in self-harming together."

A.   "True"

Kristyn takes a long drag, holds it, then exhales.

A.	"You know, it's starting to sink in how we both kept secrets from one another."

Kristyn takes another drag.

Q.	"Why did you choose to keep secrets from Maddison?"

She shrugs her shoulders.

A.	"Why do I do any of the stupid shit I do?"

Q.	"That is why I am asking."

A.	"Because I wouldn't be me if I didn't."

She waves smoke out of her face.

A.	"I'm really not in the mood to play the shame game."

Q.	"I'm sorry. What is the shame game?"

A.	"It's this thing a shrink told me."

Kristyn drops her voice a few octaves, imitating the doctor.

A.	"He said, '*Now Kristyn, with cutting comes shame. And with shame comes secrecy, isolation, alienation, depression and self-hatred.*"

She then changes her voice back to normal.

A.	"My reply was one of, "*Shut up fossil. You don't know shit 'bout self-hatred despite your sodding diplomas and textbook talk. Unless you've been in my shoes, piss-off!*"
Q.	"When did you visit with this doctor?"

A. "After Maddison died. My counselor convinced my parents I needed to talk to someone, and she recommended the bloke. I think his name was Dr. Fielding. Dr. Fester. Dr. Fuckhead. *Whatever.* All I remember is his last name began with an 'F'. I saw him a few times, then told my parents I didn't want to see him anymore. It wasn't helping. So, they let me stop going."

Kristyn releases a chuckle.

A. "He was so bloody clueless and stuck in the 1970's. You should have seen his kitschy office decor. It was something to marvel at for sure."

We're talking macramé owls hanging on the walls. I'm guessing his wife made them. Or, maybe he bought them online. Who knows? Who cares? He had an old brown leather couch. I mean, so old, it cracked like dry skin in wintertime when I sat on it. The walls were wood-paneled. There were stacks of books piled up on the floor, everywhere. I never saw so many books in one room. And the place smelled of stale cigars and mothballs.

Q. "I was going to ask if you thought the doctor was right in what he said, but you answered my question."

A. "Oh, maybe I'm telepathic. Or maybe I'm psychopathic. Haven't sorted that one out, yet. Thoughts?"

chapter forty-five

Q. "Is there a certain time of day you prefer to self-harm?"

A. "I cut when I need to. It's that simple, unlike common core math."

Why was common core math invented anyway? Talk 'bout going 'round a mountain when you could just climb straight over and save half the time.'

She mumbles.

A. *"Hate that bloody class."*

Q. "How does your math theory work regarding cutting?"

A. "Pain plus cutting equals relief."
    $(pain + cutting = relief)$

'Boom!'

Q. "How about pain plus dealing equals healing, instead?"
    $(pain + dealing = healing)$

A. "I think I like my theory better. But, *whatever.*"

Q. "Do you have a place where you prefer to self-harm?"

A. "I told you already."

Kristyn twitches her mouth side to side for her own personal amusement.

Q. "Let me clarify."

A. "You're in charge."

Q. "Do you have a safe place where you prefer to self-harm?"

She has a hint of sarcasm to her voice.

A. "Not an-*eee*-more."

Q. "Do you mind telling me where it was?"

'Yes, I mind.'

A. "My bedroom."

Q. "Why do you no longer feel safe self-harming in your bedroom?"

A. "Because t*hey* invaded it, through my laptop on social media."

'I don't like reading bad shit written 'bout myself, especially when I'm at home. But I can't stop myself from looking. Social media, to me, is now like having a bad case of gangrene. I need to sever it so it doesn't wind up destroying the rest of me…only I can't seem to find the courage to quit it.'
No sooner are those words spoken and Kristyn picks up her cell phone and

begins reading more lies spread about her on social media. She becomes angered by it and glares hard at the cruel words. She feels like throwing her phone against the wall and letting it shatter into a thousand pieces. But she refrains. Not for fear of losing control. Not for knowing it won't make their cruel words disappear. But because her mum warned her if she trashed one more phone, she would be paying for the next one.

'I'm so broke right now. Fucking wankers! I hate them so much!'

Q. "Suppose you had to pick a new safe place."

She remains fixated on her phone.

Without looking up, she fires back a curse reply.

A. "Let's not and say I did."

Q. "Where might your new safe place be?"

She looks up again wearing a faint expression of confusion this time.

A. "I don't know."

'I'm probably going to burn in hell for that lie.'

Q. "I think you do.

'My closet. Spill it, Kristyn. Brilliant! Looks like my conscience is now getting a conscience.'

A. "My closet. Happy now?"

She sneers.
Q. "Why your closet?"

A. "Because closets keep secrets hidden in the dark where they belong."

Later that Night...

(Hiding inside the Closet Cutting on her upper arm)

I'm as addicted to *cutting like* a junkie is to heroin.

I want to stop, I really do.

But I can't. It's all I have now.

No more Maddison. No more Jamey - not really.

Cutting 's all I know.

I never wanted to be like this.

But I am.

I'm soooooooooo fucking pathetic.

chapter forty-six

Q. "Do you experience feelings of arousal when self-harming?"

'What kind of fucked-up question is that? And here I thought I was the twisted one.'

A. "Never."

Kristyn takes a sip of Cherry Cola and wipes the corners of her mouth.

A. "But I do think cutting's kind of romantic."

Q. "I'm a bit intrigued. Romantic how?"

She snickers while taking another drink causing droplets of carbonation from the Cherry Cola to tickle the inside of her nose.

A. "Well, I don't see the razor blade as a Prince to come and rescue this damsel in constant distress. I'm talking 'bout the touch."

Q. "The touch?"

Kristyn smiles cunningly.
A. "That's what I said."

Q. "Explain, please."

A. "It's 'bout feeling that cool piece of metal resting against my skin as I prepare to release the monster."

She shivers.

A. 'I get goosebumps just thinking 'bout the warm rush that washes over me as my blood seeps forth from the wound, carrying with it all the pain I've been holding in. It's like I'm grieving, but at the same time, experiencing the most euphoric pleasure in my life."

Q. "What happens once the euphoria disappears?"

A sour look comes upon her face.

A. "The pain or monster returns."

She whispers.

A. *"It always does. But I can't seem to stop doing it."*

'Bugger.'

chapter forty-seven

A. "I crave it. You know?"

Q. "Self-harming?"

A. "Yes."

Q. "You can replace a negative behavior with a positive one, if you so choose."

A. "That's what I've been trying to do with all of this soul-bearing crap in these sessions. But it's not helping. I'm still cutting and doing other bad stuff to myself. Why am I like this?"

Q. "It takes time to develop healthier habits."

A. "Cutting is not a habit. It's a way of life. My life. I don't know if I can survive without doing it."

Q. "It will take work and patience on your part. You can overcome it, but you have to want to overcome it."

The fear of change causes Kristyn to invoke her defensive mechanism. She snaps back rather snidely.

A. "What if I don't *want* to overcome it."

Q.   "Kristyn, just admit it."

A.   "Admit what?"

Q.   "The self-destructive behavior you do to yourself is no longer working for you."

She shrugs her shoulders.

'I don't know what you expect me to say. I don't know what you want me to say. I don't know what to say.'

Q.   "Let me ask you something."

'I can hardly wait.'

A.   "What?"

Q.   "Do you *really* want to quit self-harming?"

A.   Do I have a choice?"

Q.   "You always have a choice."

Kristyn glances out the window.

A.   "I want the pain and self-hatred to stop. I really do. But I don't know how to silence it without silencing me. Do you know what I mean?"

'Please tell me you understand what I'm saying. Please. Because I'm not so sure I do. I only know that I want the monster to go away and never return. But how do I even try and make that happen without cutting?'

Q.   "No."

'Fantastic!'

Q.   "Are you afraid of making the same choice Maddison did if
you do not stop self-harming?"

Kristyn remains silent.

Later that night….

'I'm such a pathetic pussy, sitting here in the dark, in the closet, cutting because I can't handle my feelings 'bout Maddison right now. I miss her so much. It hurts so much. There are so many things I want to tell her, to ask her, but I know she can't hear me. I want to know why you did it Maddison. Why did you leave me?'

Two more painful cuts and still no answers. Kristyn washes up, gets into bed and cries herself to sleep while holding onto the pillow — a representation of Maddison and if she were truthful to herself…Jamey, too.

chapter forty-eight

Kristyn pulls her knees up to her chest and starts rocking back and forth. She stares straight ahead and says nothing with her lips, but everything with her eyes.

'I'm so fucking confused right now.'

Q. "You need to make some major changes in your life, Kristyn. It's time to grow up."

She becomes defensive – angry.

A. "My life is fine. I manage. Maddison was the one who couldn't handle it. She's the one who's dead, remember?

She points at herself for emphasis.

A. I'm. Still. Here."

'Unfortunately.'

Q. "Look at your wrists, Kristyn."

She does.

A. "Yeah. So?"

Q. "Do you consider those fresh cuts I see as managing your life?"

Kristyn pulls both sleeves down over her hands and then sits on them. She cannot face the truth — so she chooses to try and hide it instead.

Q. "You sit in these sessions wondering why Maddison is no longer here, and yet, you still are? I think you fear change. I think you fear letting go and embracing a new life."

'Shut-up! Shut-up! Shut-up!'

Q. "I see you trying, Kristyn."

She whispers, while staring down at the floor to avoid eye-contact.

A. "I feel nothing."

Q. "What do you want to do about it?"

A. "Cut. Vomit. Scream. Whatever. I just want to feel anything other than the nothing I'm feeling right now."

This shit I'm dealing

with now is

ALL YOUR FAULT,

Maddison!

I hate you!
No! I take it back!

I love you!
Bitch!

chapter forty-nine

Q. "What do you think of yourself? First impression. Go!"

A. *"Wait. What?"*

Q. "Do not think about it. Just say whatever comes into your head."

A. "O-okay."

Q. "What do you think of yourself? Go."

A. "A lonely naked mole rat."

Q. "Why a lonely naked mole rat?"

'Because the resemblance is undeniable. Duh!'

A. "I'm alone in the dark, hidden from the rest of the world, too ugly to look at or love."

chapter fifty

It is a rainy day. And rainy days mean only one thing to Kristyn. Depression. She arrives to the session soaking wet; matted hair, runny make-up and in a dreary mood. She had deliberately left her umbrella behind in her school locker.

'I was hoping the rain would wash the icky feelings I have 'bout myself away. Didn't work. I look and feel shittier than before. If that's even possible. Which based on how I'm feeling, apparently is.'

She sits down in the red chair and then shakes her hair a few times with her hands hoping it will dry quicker.

Q. "You seem bothered more than usual."

A. "Why do you say that?"

Q. "Because you came in soaked from the rain and you are wearing a look of misery upon your face."

She wrings more rain out of her shirt.

A. "What the fuck have I got to smile 'bout? *Huh?*"

Q. "What in particular has you so upset right now?"
She says nothing.

Q. "Okay. Let's try this question. What are you feeling?"

A. "Disgust."

Q. "At whom?"

A. "Myself."

Q. "Why?"

A. "I don't like learning the truth 'bout myself since doing these sessions. I'd rather know nothing, be nothing and do nothing. I've gotten pretty good at it."

Kristyn pulls out an ink pen and begins drawing small frowning faces on the palm of her left hand.

Q. "Why are you drawing sad faces on your hand?"

She doesn't look up. She merely mumbles a reply while drawing an upside-down smile.

A. *"I feel sad inside."*

Q. "Why do you feel sad?"

A. "You keep making me talk 'bout myself. I hate talking 'bout myself. I told you that the first day."

Q. "I know you find talking about yourself uncomfortable and I am sorry. But..."

A. "No, you're not."

Q.   "You will not always feel this way, Kristyn."

Kristyn draws a giant sad face over the little ones and then holds up her hand. She then tosses the pen onto the table.

A.   "I don't believe you."

chapter fifty-one

Q. "When you self-harm…"

A. "I told you everything already."

Q. "Aside from pain release and the occasional euphoria, how else do you feel after self-harming?"

A. "How does a carrot feel after being cut?"

Q. "Be serious, please."

'Buggering hell. What do you want from me? I've told you what you wanted to hear, mixed in with what I felt like sharing at the time you asked. And, yet, here you are, wanting more. Will any of my answers ever be enough for you? Will you ever be satisfied with anything I say? Ever?'

A. "Sometimes I feel better. Sometimes I feel worse. Sometimes I feel pissed off. Sometimes I feel shame. Lately though, I've felt…*nothing.*"

Q. "What causes you to feel anger after self-harming?"

A. "Sometimes it's the situation."
That wretched moment with Ian Rhodes in the garage for example. It's amazing what a little MDMA and a moment of low self-esteem can

make one feel weak enough to do. Blech!'

A. "Sometimes I get mad at myself for being so frail."

'I want to kick myself in my stale, stank fanny when I get a moment of weakness like that. But I never muster up the nerve to do it. To be honest, I'd probably get off on the pain. Wow! That sounds so sad….and really fucked up. But it's the unfortunate truth — for once.'

A.   "Sometimes I get mad because it didn't help at all."

'Contrary to what most non-cutters think, being a cutter really sucks. It's hard living with something inside of you that's capable of making you feel so worthless; you harm yourself on purpose just to feel something other than the shitty, emotional way you are feeling in that moment.'

Q. "I am optimistic you will eventually overcome self-harming."

'Good luck.'

A.   "You do realize you are speaking to an obvious pessimistic, right?"

Note to Self...

Yeah, I hate me, too.

chapter fifty-two

Q. "Are you still seeing your school counselor on a regular basis?"

Kristyn scratches an itch on her left shoulder.

A. "I check in with her once a month now."

Q. "Does talking to her help?"

A. "We mostly talk 'bout my shitty grades. I don't want to discuss anything else with her."

Q. "Any particular reason why?"

A. "Anything I say she'll run tell my parents."

Q. "I see."

'Glad you do…for once.'

Q. "How have you been feeling lately about what happened with Maddison?"

A. "I still struggle to get out of bed some days because I can't handle the pain of missing her so much and still partly blaming myself for not being a better friend."

She becomes pithy.

A. "Other days I'm really angry at her."

Q. "You sound a bit angry now."

A. "I am."

Q. "Why are you angry?"

Kristyn crosses her arms.

A. "Because if she hadn't decided to check out, I wouldn't be here forced to talk 'bout my own shit."

Q. "Instead of focusing on the anger…"

A. "Don't tell me not to be angry. I have every right to be angry at her."

Q. "I am not negating your feelings, Kristyn. I want you to set your focus on the good that is coming out of such a tragic event."

A. "What good? Maddison's dead and I'm being forced to talk 'bout myself. Which I hate doing."

Q. "But you are getting the help you need. The help you want."

She becomes sarcastic.

A. "Am I?"

Q. "Why do you seem to view getting help as something negative?"

Kristyn suddenly drops her head and whispers.

A. *"Because I'm still here and she's not."*

Q. "Maddison made a choice, Kristyn. You did, too."

A. "Choice? *Pah!* It doesn't feel that way."

Q. "How does it feel, then?"

A. "Like I had no choice. That's how."

chapter fifty-three

Q. "Are you ready to talk to your parents yet about the issues you are dealing with?"

A. "What if I tell them and it makes them stop loving me or never look at me the same way again? Then what?"

Q. "How do you think your parents look at you now?"

I'm sure they would be super proud to know their daughter drinks, does drugs, has sex with random boys. Oh, and mutilates her body. There's something to brag 'bout at the next High School Reunion.'

Q. "Are you afraid your parents love for you will change if they learn the truth?"

A. "I know my parents love me. I do. But I don't know if they could handle it. I know I can't and I'm the one that's doing it to myself."

chapter fifty-four

Q. "Do you feel alienated, Kristyn?"

Kristyn lights up a cigarette.

'If you were me, you'd feel alienated along with a few other things. Trust me. Oh, wait. On second thought. Don't trust me. Hell, I don't even trust me. I lie to everyone 'bout everything…including myself.'

A. "Duh."

She tosses the lighter onto the table.

Q. "Who makes you feel alienated?"

A. "The entire world."

Q. "That seems a bit extreme, don't you think?"

She takes a drag before answering.

A. "Not really."

Q. "Have you seen the entire world, yet?"

'Surely you must know I was being ironic with my answer.'

A. "I can't imagine it being any better, unless you know something I don't."

Q. "If that is what you choose to think."

A. "How many times are you going bring up the choice crap?"

Q. "If you want to see making choices as a bad thing then...."

She moves her right index finger in a circular motion devoid of excitement.

A. *"Yeah. Yeah. I know. My choice."*

chapter fifty-five

Q. "Who do you think you are in this world?"

A. "God's perfect little joke."

Q. "Always quick to speak the worst about yourself."

A. "Can you blame me?"

Q. "You are not here by accident. Your life has meaning, Kristyn. It has purpose. Did you ever consider that maybe God is going to help you to help others someday?"

She wears a skeptical expression upon her face.

A. "Why me?"

Q. "I think a better question to ask is 'why not you'?"

chapter fifty-six

No show.
The digital recorder was left on in case Kristyn decided to make an appearance.
She never did.

Instead she...

Kristyn chose to blow off the session and spend time hiding inside her closet and cutting after seeing a photo on social medial of Jamey and Jinger making out.

"Thank you for breaking my heart and rubbing it in, Jamey. oh, and FUCK YOU, TOO, YOU TWATWAFFLE!"

Later that night she went to her favorite dance club. After paying off the bouncer with some spliff, she ran into her MDMA hottie.

"Toby? Tanner? Tank? Tosser? Whatever. He always gives me good shit to help erase Jamey from my memory."

Jamey was far off from her memory, as she danced wildly to the bass music pumping, until a familiar pair of hands found their way around her waist from behind. The moment she felt a pair of lips touch her neck, followed by the combined smell of sweat, alcohol and cologne, she knew it was Jamey.

"I should have punched him the dick straight away. But I didn't. My stupid heart was overcome with emotion just being in his arms again. we danced and kissed and danced some more under the flashing lights. It was exhilarating. It felt like old times - like we had never been apart. Jamey. The MDMA. All of it. Until..."

Jamey suddenly pushed Kristyn away and acted as if he did not know her when Jinger walked into the club. He immediately left a very heartbroken and confused Kristyn alone on the dance floor. Through the flashing strobe light, Kristyn saw Jamey and Jinger pressed up against the wall in a mad make-out session.

I screamed "FUCKING TOSSER!" at the top of my lungs, but Jamey didn't hear me. Nobody heard me. The music was too loud. I couldn't believe I let him headfuck me AGAIN! WHY ARE YOU SOOOOO STUPID, KRISTYN??????????

A few hours and five shots of Tequila later, found Kristyn and her MDMA hottie getting hot and heavy locked inside a bathroom stall in the men's loo. Too bad she learned rough sex pressed up against a wall peppered with loose girls' phone numbers and tacky limericks, a previous emotional ride with the boy who has your heart, plus several shots of Tequila do not mix well.

"At least Ted? Tom? Ty? Tosser? Whatever, didn't bail once I started my sickening 'retch-a-thon'. He stayed and held my hair back like a gentleman while I puked up tequila, along with my feelings for Jamey, for the next thirty-minutes. Nice bloke for sure. Feel like a shit though because I can't remember his name. Seems odd to ask it of him since we've shagged, I don't know how many times now."

The next morning, with a hangover from hell, Kristyn truly wished she were dead for she felt pain like no other not only in her head, but still in her heart.

"Te-killa! Never again!"

chapter fifty-seven

Kristyn places an index finger on each corner of her mouth and then pulls them up to form an over-exaggerated smile.

A. "Look! I'm smiling."

Q. "Let's talk about your anxiety attacks."

She immediately pulls her smile back into a frown.

A. "They suck."

'The end.'

Q. "Is there a particular trigger that brings on your anxiety attacks?"

She looks around the room and notices the spider plant is gone.

'If you keep talking 'bout my anxiety, my stupid brain is probably going to launch into an attack. You've been warned.'

A. "Life."

Q. "What do you experience during an anxiety attack?"
A. "I don't know how to explain it."

Q. "Try."

A. "I sweat. I feel like I'm going to puke. My heart pounds so hard it hurts my chest. I wring my hands so tight; I almost break the bones in my fingers. I breathe really fast, too. It's like I want to have control, but my body and mind won't listen. So, I suffer through it until it stops. I pretty much feel helpless to stop anything or control anything happening in my life at all."

chapter fifty-eight

A. "Yeah, so a while back my school counselor, Mrs. Duvayne started questioning me 'bout Maddison's habits."

Q. "What sort of habits did she want to know about?"

A. "Apparently, Maddison's parents gave her journal to Mrs. Duvayne. I guess they wanted answers for why she did what she did and thought I could help. Maybe they wanted to know if they were to blame somehow. I don't know."

Q. "Do you blame Maddison's parents for Maddison's death?"

A. "No."

She rubs her sweaty palms on her jeans.

A. "At first I blamed the bullies for what they did to her and then myself. I mean, I still do, just not as much."

Q. "So, who do you blame now?"

A. "Maddison."

Q. "Really."

A. "Yeah. I'm starting to understand Maddison was going to most likely do what she did regardless. I'm just guessing. I don't really know. I'm not a shrink. I'm just a kid, you know?"

chapter fifty-nine

A. "After meeting with Mrs. Duvayne, I learned Maddison not only journaled her cutting, but she also took mini-polaroids of the cuts and then taped them in the same journal. What the fuck was she thinking?"

Q. "Did you ever journal your own self-harming behavior?"

A. "I have journaled in the past 'bout cutting, but I never took pictures. Never!"

Q. "Did you see the pictures of Maddison's cuts?"

A. "Yes, after getting permission from Maddison's parent's and my parent's, too."

Q. "How did you feel seeing the pictures of Maddison's self-harming behavior?"

A. "Sick."

Q. "Why?"

A. "I felt like I was looking at myself in a mirror."

Q. "You saw yourself in Maddison's photos?"

A. "Yes."

Q. "Did seeing the photos help lessen your desire to self-harm?"

A. "Oddly, it made the urge to want to cut stronger."

Q. "Did you ever provide Maddison's parent's any answers to their questions, especially after seeing the pictures and reading her journal?"

A. "No."

Q. "Why not?"

'Because after reading her journal, turns out, I didn't really know Maddison at all. It's so messed up. She was my best friend. How could that happen?'

A. "I didn't want to betray her. I still don't."

chapter sixty

A. "Sometimes I get a rush from cutting and it's the best feeling in the world when it happens. But…"

Q. "But?"

A. "Coming down can feel even worse."

Q. "What do you feel coming down from a self-harming high?"

A. "Unbearable pain."

Q. "From the wound you caused?"

A. "That, too."

Q. "What do you mean, that too?"

A. "Sometimes there is lingering emotional pain I didn't realize I blocked out that suddenly appears without warning."

Q. "What do you do when that happens?"

A. "I cut again. I'm basically seeking more endorphins like a junkie."

Q. "Does it work?"

A. "Not really."

Q. "So why continue doing it?"

A. "Because my head is all messed up at the time. I'm in physical pain from having to cut deeper. And I'm now feeling emotionally frustrated with the forgotten feelings I uncovered."

chapter sixty-one

Kristyn snidely raises her eyebrows and then takes a drag off her cigarette.

Q. "You do realize you are only hurting yourself with risky behavior like self-harm, drink, drugs and cigarettes, right?"

'Take your judgmental attitude and shove it.'

She takes another drag and blows smoke rings.

A. "That's the point."

Q. "Have you considered seeking other ways to feel better?"

A. "I tried running once."

Q. "And?"

A. "I got a cramp on my side and felt like shit afterwards. The 'high' felt nothing like the kind I get from cutting."

Q. "Maybe you did not give running a chance. You said you only tried it once."

A. "I hate exercising."

Q. "Exercise is good for your health."

A.   "So are strawberries. But I'm allergic, so not happening."

About Last Night....

"Stupid, Kristyn! Why are you so fucking dumb and pathetic? Huh? Why do you insist on doing stupid shit that is going to hurt you? Why did you look at Jamey's page? Why? He's happy now with Jinger. Get over it will you! Stop letting him headfuck you! Please! Idiot!!!!!!!"

"Yeah, so after bashing myself verbally for still getting upset over Jamey being with Jinger and feeling no relief, I crawled into my closet. Of course, I had to wait until my parents crashed out to avoid getting caught. So, yeah, I cut. The good news? It wasn't that deep of a cut this time. Maybe that means I'm starting to finally get over Jamey, huh? I hope so."

"What sucked though is I grew bored waiting for the teeny tiny amount of blood to seep out from the cut. So, I made the mistake of looking up. That's when I saw the dress hanging there. You know – the one Maddison and I had been working on before she hung herself in her closet. Yeah, so my mind started fucking with me. The dress became her. I saw her hanging there. Sad and alone in the dark. I freaked out and bolted out of the closet. I could barely catch my breath. I had chills running up and down my arms and legs. It was surreal. I mean, really."

"Seth hit me up. All I could think was, "How did he know I needed a distraction?" I really wasn't in the mood to 'party'. But then again, I was so freaked out over Jamey and seeing Maddison, I hit him back and we hooked up."

"I met Seth at a park nearby. We dropped MDMA and played around on the slides and swings and stuff. Oh, and we did some naughty, but fun stuff, too. I always have a good time with Seth. FWB's is the way to go. That's what I tell myself in the moment. But come morning, I always feel like cheap, used up shit. And yet, the next time I need a distraction or to feel something, I do it again. I'm so fucked up!!!!!!!!"

chapter sixty-two

Q. "Is the physical pain you cause worth the emotional pain you seek to escape from?"

'Well, duh!'

A. "I hate that I cut, but like I've said before, I can't quit. Sometimes I'll lay in bed at night staring up at the bedroom ceiling and question myself."

Q. "What do you question about yourself?"

A. "Why do I *really* cut? I mean, aside from the reasons I've already given. How did I *really* get here? Where did I go wrong?"

Q. "The fact that you recognize this issue is a good start towards finding the answer you seek."

A. *"Cheers"*

Goodbye old Friend

A month has passed by since Kristyn's last session. Unfortunate circumstances caused her to crawl into a metaphoric cocoon. She simply could not handle life anymore. She also could not handle coming close to learning the answer, the truth behind her desire to self-harm. Since then, she has been unable to see any light ahead. Only a road paved in endless darkness.

Jamey 'the twatwaffle' Marotto did not fail to disappoint once again in the headfucking department. Although he's going out with Jinger, he rang Kristyn up one night out of the blue. He asked to meet her at the park where they used to spend most of their 'private time'. Jamey's the type of bloke who enjoys taking risks - cheating on tests as well as partners.

Jamey told Kristyn he wanted to discuss getting back together for real this time. He said he was not happy with Jinger. She was a bore. And shagging her was like putting his willy into the knot hole on a two by four plank.

Kristyn was so excited. She put on her sexiest top and jeans and fixed her hair. She looked stunning for a girl who had been put through a mountain of shit over the last year by the Jamey and Maddison drama. She was so excited to be getting back together with Jamey, again. It was something she had been wishing for since the day he told her to "Piss off!" without reason.

Hours ticked by as Kristyn sat alone on the swing set,

in the cool breeze, making endless excuses inside her head as to why Jamey had not shown up, yet;

"His mum wouldn't let him leave so he had to wait for her to nod off."
"He was finishing up homework and lost track of time."
"one of his mates was in trouble so he had to go help them."

Eventually, the reality Jamey had headfucked her once more finally hit. A storm had blown in by this time. Kristyn walked back to her flat, head down, crying, shoes in hand, getting soaked in the pouring rain. It was hard to differentiate between her tears and raindrops. She prayed lightning would strike her. unfortunately, God failed to answer that prayer.

By the time she reached home, Kristyn accepted it was finally over. Why Jamey kept messing with her head and her heart all this time, especially when he was the one who first ended things, she did not understand.

"Sick, fucking, twisted, bastard! I'm done stroking his ego and his pathetic wee willy! She can have him!"

The following week, Kristyn learned through a social media posting on Jamey's page that he and Jinger were super serious. More than he ever was with Kristyn. He claimed Jinger to be the 'love of his life'. After reading and re-reading the post twenty times, Kristyn flew into a self-harming frenzy. She quit attending her sessions and shut down emotionally - only leaving her room to go to school.

"Bloody tosser! He knew how much I loved him. He just used me to boost his ego. I hate having to see the two of them making-out in the hallway at school like guppies on dry-land gasping for air. But if I stay home, mum will be up my fanny like a cheap, cardboard coated, petrol station tampon, giving me nothing but grief and being a pain. I can't deal with her shit on top of Jamey's shit, on top of my own shit. So, I have to suck it up and go to prison. Sorry, I mean, school where all I do is count down the minutes until the final bell rings and I am paroled."

Day after day, Kristyn would come home and retreat to her room where she would cry, cut, binge, purge, blast dark-depressing music and sleep. Later, after her parents crashed out, she would sneak out of the house and drop MDMA, go dancing, and sometimes shag Seth or the MDMA hottie.

Morning would always find Kristyn passed out on her bed wearing the same clothes from the night before or naked if she snuck a guy home with her. A trashcan would be close by in case she had to vomit upon waking up. As always, the bright sun would arrive, stinging her eyes something awful through the window.

"Fucking ball of yellow shit", she would often shout out, before pulling the duvet up over her head.

"I mean, what idiot came up with that annoying phrase...'ball of sunshine'. Seriously? What is there to like 'bout the sun. All it means is another day of more depressing crap."

Today, she awoke feeling shitty. No surprise. Last night was rough. First, she saw Jamey and Jinger glued at the lips in the club. Then, Seth ended their FwB's because he had met someone. Kristyn didn't really care, as far as her heart. Seth was just a guy she shagged here and there. But he wasn't going to be available to use as a distraction to forget Jamey when she needed to, anymore. It sent her into a panic. That moment of weakness and despair found Kristyn hooking-up with Ian Rhodes in the backseat of his car.

"What the fuck, Kristyn?" was all she could utter after climbing out and walking home sipping on a fifth of liquor she nicked from underneath the passenger seat in Ian's car.

After getting up, taking a piss and brushing her teeth, she stopped and stared at herself in the mirror.

"I felt like I had hit rock bottom before. But seeing Jamey paw the shit out of Jinger after he talked 'bout getting back together with me, made me feel like rock bottom with ten boulders tossed on top. I mean, how could I have ever been so daft to love someone who never really loved me at all? And, Ian, again. why??????"

She sticks her tongue out at her reflection. Her rank morning breath could wake the dead.

"Fucking worthless bitch. No wonder he doesn't want you."

She half-combs her hair and runs a line of extra-thick black eyeliner under each eye, before smearing it. The purpose? To hide the redness in her eyes from purging after coming home from the club. She throws a casual glance at the trashcan filled with empty Twinkie wrappers and a crushed-up cereal box.

"Whatever."

She exits the bathroom and wanders over to a pile of dirty clothes. After rifling through them, she decides to wear her black 'Slip Knot' burnout T shirt and a pair of baggy blue jeans.

"Jamey always said I never had much of an ass. Suppose it was because he was the ass in our relationship. If you can even call it that. A trip to see a gyno named Dr. Claw would have been less painful."

Today, for some reason, Kristyn woke-up feeling different. Maybe it was because she feared her teeth might rot and fall out if she purged one more night. Maybe she feared a blood transfusion if she cut and bled anymore. Or maybe she was just sick and tired or feeling sick and tired. She walked back into the bathroom to REALLY face herself in the mirror for the first time and get honest.

"You dozy cow. All you've been doing this past month is hurting yourself. Don't you get it? Jamey doesn't give a shit if you live or die. Maddison, either or she'd still be here. Nor do the Posh Miss Perfects - as if I give a fuck what those twats think 'bout me. But, whatever."

She takes a deep breath and exhales.

"Why are you locked away in your room, crying, binging, purging and cutting yourself to death? For what? Him? Her? Them? Snap the fuck out of it, girl! Seriously! It's not working anymore. None of it."

"Who the fuck is Jamey Marotto anyway? Nothing. A nobody. A zero. A twatwaffle who can't shag worth a damn. Who is Maddison? She was your best friend, but she's gone now. It's time to let her go. And the Posh Miss Perfects can piss off!"

Kristyn decides to make the boldest move of her life. She throws her razor blade in the trash. Yes, the same blade she always carried in her purse. The same blade that had seen her through some pretty fucked up times. The same blade that had been sitting on her sink, with blood still on it, from the night before.

The razor blade lands on top of the numerous plastic crinkled wrappers and a crushed-up cereal box.

"No more cutting. I mean it, girl. No more shagging. No more binging. No more purging. No more burning. No more starving yourself. No more hitting yourself. No more doing anything shitty to yourself."

She watches as the razor blade, her metaphoric teddy bear, helplessly sinks into the sea of empty wrappers. For a moment, she feels the urge to retrieve it. But refrains.

"Don't you even think 'bout pulling it out of the bin you stupid bitch. I mean it."

She stares down at it, still fighting the urge to save it.

"I'm going to quit you. I know I will. I just can't give you that kind of power over my life anymore. I can't give Jamey that kind of power either. He broke my heart once. Twice. Three times. Hell, a million times. I refuse to give him the chance to make it one-million and one. And I refuse to let you, my dear razor, who has always been there for me in my time of need, to be there for me anymore while I heal from Maddison, either. I can't. I have to do this on my own."

And so...Kristyn decided it was time to resume her sessions.

"I can do this. I am going to do this. I know it's the right thing for me to do."

Then, a moment of doubt creeps in.
"Right?"

She stares into the bin once more, hoping for confirmation from her old friend that she is in fact, making the right choice for once in her life. The razor blade appears to answer, as it slowly disappears from her sight, as the plastic wrappers finally give way to the weight of it.

chapter sixty-three

Q.   "How long has it been since you last cut?"

'Come on, girl. You can do this.'

She answers in a meek tone.

A.   *"Seven days."*

'Way to proudly own your progress, idiot! Seven days is seven days more than before.'

Q.   "That is great news, Kristyn."

Kristyn half-smiles.

A.   "You actually believe me?"

Q.   "Is there any reason I should doubt you?"

A.   "I mean, it's been a month since we talked."

Q.   "I know. I have been worried about you."

She feels ashamed for her recent out-of-control behavior.
A.   "To be honest, I was worried 'bout me, too."

She stares down at her covered wrists before looking back up.

A.   "Are you sure you don't want me to like pull up my sleeves or lift my shirt or something and make sure I'm not lying?"

Q.   "I trust you."

'Okay. Now I'm getting scared because I'm a notorious fuck up. How am I ever going to pull off not fucking up? How?'

A.   "What if I become weak and cut again? Then I've failed right?"

Q. "If you happen to self-harm again, do not consider it a failure. Failing is a part of life. Not everyone succeeds the first time they try. The important thing is to try again."

She ponders the statement while reaching into her purse to seek comfort from her stainless-steel friend, before remembering she threw it away.

'I miss you, mate. Why did I toss you in the bin? I'm not sure I did the right thing by letting you go.'

A.   "I don't know if I can do this."

There is a sudden knock at the door. The digital audio voice recorder is turned off.

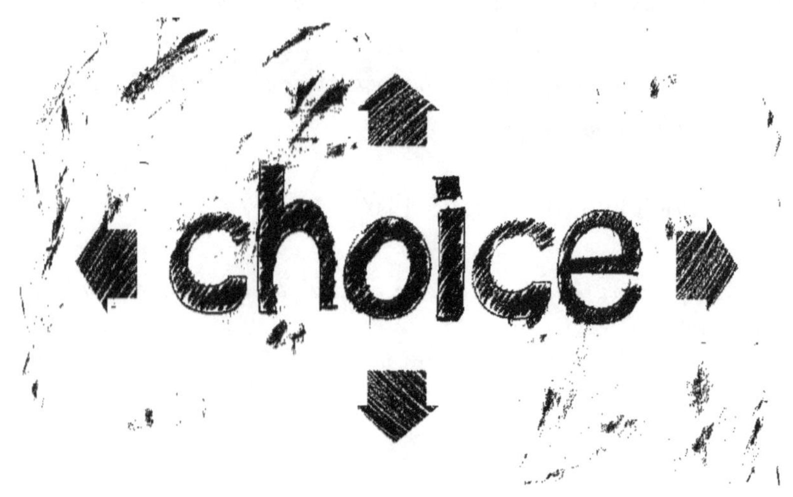

Bugger! what should I do???????
Help!!!!!!

K.   "Come in."

Kristyn's mum enters Kristyn's bedroom and finds her daughter sitting in a faded-red antique wing armchair placed before a full-length mirror hanging on the wall. She is quick to notice several empty soda cans, a pack of cigarettes, Kristyn's purse and a digital recorder sitting on a small, medium height table next to the mirror.

M. "Morning, sweetheart."

Kristyn lightly mutters a reply.

K. "Hey, mum."

M. "Breakfast will be ready soon. I made your favorite. Blueberry pancakes."

Her mum glances over at a digital clock resting on an end table beside Kristyn's bed.

M. "You need to hurry up, sweetie, and get ready for school or you'll be late."

Kristyn's mum walks over and begins making the bed. Kristyn stands up and grabs the digital audio voice recorder off the table. She takes a deep breath. Her heart and mind are racing at equal pace as an argument begins happening inside her head.

'You can do this.'
'No, I can't.'
'Yes, you can.'
'You have to.'
'Don't be such a pussy.'

Kristyn knows she must make a choice.

'It is now or never, bitch!'

She looks at herself in the mirror in disgust. Messy hair and dark circles are not helping paint a better picture. Strong waves of emotion wash over her. She feels like throwing-up. Her gut tells her to speak-up. But should she trust it? Can she trust it?

'Go on then. Tell her. What are you waiting for? A red carpet to roll out?'

She tries to take a step forward, but then hesitates and remains frozen in place. She whispers under her breath.

'Chicken shit.'

She looks at her wretched reflection in the mirror again for reassurance only to find it staring back at her just as unsure.

'Fuck it. You have to do this, or you'll never get better.'

Kristyn's mum is busy fluffing a pillow on the bed.

K.   "Mum?"

Her mum looks up and immediately notices a look of sadness in her daughter's eyes.

M.   "What's the matter, darling? Is it Jamey, again?"

K.   "No. Well, yes. I mean, no."

She hedges before pointing at the bed.
K.   "Can you sit down? Please."

Her mum sits down on the bed.

'No going back now.'

K.   "I need to tell you something, mum. It's something…"

M.   "Is everything okay, sweetie?"

Kristyn then places the digital audio voice recorder with all of her 'sessions' into her mum's hand and then rolls up the sleeves on her shirt, exposing the many cuts and scars on her wrists.

A.   "No."

The End

Note from the Author

Self-harming is not an uncommon occurrence. It is not considered to be a mental illness either, but rather a negative behavior that happens when there is an inability to manage stresses in life.

Mental health illnesses often associated with self-harming are; borderline personality disorder, eating disorders, posttraumatic distress disorder, depression and anxiety. But again, self-harming itself is not a mental illness. It is a negative coping mechanism.

There are crisis centers, doctors and therapists who can help you overcome self-harming behavior. There is no shame in reaching out for help, nor is there shame in being a self-harmer.

Bad stuff happens to us sometimes. It's life. When it does, we all have a way of handling it. But sometimes those ways are not healthy for us. They are damaging; physically, mentally, and emotionally.

Being a self-harmer does not mean you are a weak person who cannot deal with life. You just need some guidance, reassurance and support while learning how to better manage issues in life.

According to Dr. Caroline Leaf, *"75% to 95% of the illnesses that plague us today are a direct result of our thought life."*

How we think and what we think greatly impact us mentally, emotionally, and physically.

We detox our bodies by fasting or eating healthier. But we often forget to detox our brain. The most vital, key element in our body. The brain controls everything in the body. Research has shown a direct connection between negative thoughts and unforgiveness with cancer, diabetes, allergies, etc.

The brain needs to be detoxed from negative thoughts.

So, how does one detox their brain? By changing your thinking. You have control over what you think. You have the power. True, random thoughts can come into your brain. When they do, you have the power of choice. To accept that negative thought or reject it.

For example; *"Nothing goes right for me."*

Do you choose to accept that thought or reject it?

Your choice.

You can change your thinking and change your life. You can overcome being a self-harmer. You've got this…when, you are ready!

Glossary

Barmy:

slightly crazy, very foolish

Batty:

insane, crazed

Bloke:

guy

Bloody:

swear word

Bloody Hell:

swear word

Bollocks:

nonsense

Bugger:

when something goes wrong, jerk

Buggering Hell:

swear word

Bum:

butt

Cheeky:

spunky, sassy

Cheers:

thank you, goodbye

Cocked it up:

something done wrong or badly

Crikey:

an expression of surprise

Daft:

stupid, silly

Dozy Cow:

stupid, annoying woman

Duvet:

bedding cover filled with down, feathers

Fanny:

female genitalia

Flat:

apartment

Fuck's sake:

anger, frustration

Fuckwit:

clueless, no wits

FWB:

friends with benefits

Git:

silly, senile

Gutted:

unhappy, disappointed

Headfuck:

someone who knows you love them and strings you along to mess with your head

Kick off:

start a fight, argument

Kitschy:

bad taste (art/thing/person)

Knickers:

panties

Knob head:

obnoxious person

Lager:
beer

Loo:
toilet

Masochist:
person who enjoys pain or humiliation

Mate:
friend

Mum:
mom

Nick:
steal, take

Petrol Station:
gas station

Piss Off:
leave, go away

Pissed off our faces:
drunk

Posh:
classy, fancy, spiffy

Proper:
genuine, real

Rubbish:
trash, garbage

Shagging:
sexual intercourse

Shirk:
avoid, neglect

Slag:
slut

Smarted Off:
to show disrespect verbally

Sodding:
damned, fucking, used to emphasize anger or annoyance

Sorted:
dealt with

Spliff:
marijuana joint

STFU:
shut the fuck up

Tits up:
inoperative, broken

Tosser:
idiot, braggard

Trainers:
sneakers

Twat:
obnoxious, stupid

Twatwaffle:
idiot, dumbass

Wanker:
jerk, dolt

Wee Willy:
small penis

Also, by Normandy D. Piccolo

Bullied Dying to Fit In

Each year, approximately 4,400 children commit suicide due to bullying. *Bullied Dying to Fit In* is every bullied person's story and needs to be heard. Will you listen? The book captures the raw emotional side of bullying. Though everyone's bully story is different, the pain felt is the same. The broken heart tells the tale. *Bullied Dying to Fit In* takes the bullied, the non-bullied and even the bully on an emotional roller-coaster of tears, insight, and triumph. For Teens, Parents, School Counselors & Teachers.

Bullied: Dying to Fit In was nominated and received the **Advocacy/Social Justice Award for the 2019 In the Margins Book Award/ School Library Journal**

Visit **www.normandydpiccolo.com** for more information.

About Normandy D. Piccolo

Hello. I am Normandy D. Piccolo. I am a published writer, book reviewer, advertising copywriter and freelance journalist. I have written several books, appeared on TV Talk Shows and in Mom Blogs, written radio scripts for the "Click It or Ticket" national campaign featuring Charlie Daniels and The Chicks (formally known as the Dixie Chicks). I have also written radio/TV scripts for St. Jude Children's Research Hospital. I was also nominated for a D&AD Award for my work on "Operation Lifesaver".

My song, "My Bestfriend Ted", received continuous airplay on Chicago radio. Additionally, I worked on the GodSpeaks Billboard campaign contributing campaign concepts, along with scripts for the televised cartoon, Auto-B-Good. I am a participant of the Hillsborough County Anti-Bullying Advisory Committee. My latest book, Bullied: Dying to Fit In was nominated and received the Advocacy / Social Justice Award for the 2019 In the Margins Book Award.

My book 'Why is Kristyn A. Kutter?' won two awards and was placed in the TOP 10 List for Fiction/Non-Fiction and the Fiction Recommendation List for 2021 by In the Margins Book Award / School Library Journal.

"Normandy D. Piccolo has her finger on the issues that marginalized youth must face in this society. Having previous been listed on our Social Justice Advocacy list for her nonfiction title Bullied: Dying to Fit In, her talent once again demanded the committee's attention with the no-holds-barred Why is Kristyn a Kutter? In this book the reader is served a triple play on words with the title of this book, the protagonist's name, and the issues of self-hate, self-mutilation, and depression presented in this gripping book-in-verse-narrative. Instead of talking about her problems, Kristyn A. Kutter's rebellious spirit and self-hate has led to episodes of depression and self-mutilation when things go wrong. It didn't help that her best friend committed suicide, leaving her to wonder if she will end up the same way. This book is recommended for older teens ages 16 and up and arms the reader with resources for crisis intervention through national centers and online support sites." - In the Margins Book Award Committee

Additional information, including radio, magazine, and TV interviews, can be seen at www.normandydpiccolo.com

Why is Kristyn A. Kutter?
Book Summary

Instead of talking about her problems, Kristyn A. Kutter's rebellious spirit and self-hate has led to episodes of depression and self-mutilation when things go wrong. It did not help that her best friend committed suicide, leaving her to wonder if she will end up the same way. This book arms the reader with resources for crisis intervention through national centers and online support sites.

***Trigger Warning:** Includes strong language, non-graphic depictions of self-harm, drug and alcohol usage and sexual situations. Recommended for ages 16+*.